THROUGH THE DARKNESS

STACEY WILK

TITLE
Copyright © 2019 by Stacey Wilk
Cover design copyright © 2023 by Jen Talty
ISBN: (ebook edition) 978-0-9896128-8-3
ISBN: (paperback edition) 978-0-9896128-9-0

Printed in the USA
Through the Darkness

This book is dedicated to firefighters everywhere. Thank you for your service and bravery.

CHAPTER ONE

*P*hoenix Egan should've sent a mayday call sooner. Standing inside a burning building wasn't the same as fighting a fire in the movies. No real firefighter would be able to see where he or she was going. He had trained hundreds of times for this moment, but his heart still took off like a Jet Ski. His oxygen tank would deplete faster if he didn't calm down, and then he'd really be screwed.

He couldn't see a thing. Blackness met him at every turn. The kind of darkness that swallowed up whatever was around and made it disappear forever. His oxygen tank beeped with the deafening alert of running out. Running out of air. Running out of time. He was trapped somewhere inside one of his town's two elementary schools.

The last radio call stated all the students were out, but a pet rabbit had been left behind. He had been at that section of the school and arrogant enough to believe he could find the rabbit. Instead, he had lost the handline.

With the oxygen ticking down and the smoke blocking his sight, he needed to find a door or window. He also didn't want his guys to bust his ass for freaking out when someone could be standing ten feet from him. As the captain of the company he needed to remain calm.

His hand slid over a door frame. He searched for the knob and pulled. Two steps in he collided with shelves. Not a way out. A closet. His heart continued to hammer away at his chest, and his lungs fought the short bursts of air he tried to swallow. Panic set in like a bad storm off the ocean, but he couldn't afford the use of energy. He willed his heart to slow and for ice water to run through his veins. The oxygen wasn't gone. Yet. But the tank kept sounding the alarm.

"Phoenix, where are you?" Hawk's voice crackled through the radio.

He just needed three more minutes, and he'd be fine. The door or window was around here somewhere. Hawk would have to wait for a response.

"Captain Egan, please state your location immediately." Hawk's words came through as if his jaw was clenched. His younger brother was trying to remain professional on the radio line and not doing a good job of it.

If he ran out of oxygen, he'd be a dead man. The room filled with increasing heat from the fire that had started in the cafeteria. Once the tank emptied, the instinct was to pull it off for air. If he did that, he'd only manage to burn his lungs instantly. Yeah, he was pretty much fucked in about two minutes.

"Damn it, Phoenix. Where are you? I'm coming."

"I'll figure it out." Somehow. He should be shouting mayday, but he didn't want Hawk coming for him. Anyone but Hawk.

Stupid. Of course, Hawk would respond first. He carried the guilt of losing Wyatt like a fifth limb. If anything happened to Hawk because he had to come rescue his sorry ass, it would be Phoenix's fault. He couldn't let that happen. Hawk finally had his life together.

"Like hell you will figure it out by yourself." Hawk's words were labored. He was probably trying to run back into the building and through all the smoke. So much for wanting to keep his brother safe.

Phoenix needed to find the damn classroom door. The hose line was right outside it. He dropped to his knees in hopes of gaining some visibility. He bumped into a desk.

Glass shattered in the distance. A crash and bang shook the room. The roof collapsed right behind him. He froze.

"Captain Egan, can you respond?" Chief Wylie's voice jolted him out of his space.

The door was around here somewhere. "I'm fine, Chief."

"Bullshit." Hawk again.

Voices called out over the radio. His crew scrambled, trying to save him. His head hurt. The beeping on his tank picked up speed right along with his heart. Where the fuck was the door?

He crawled across the floor, pushing desks and chairs out of his way. The visibility was maybe four inches. He could be crawling right back to that closet and not know it.

The radio hissed and cracked. The chief called Hawk back to the front of the building. Phoenix hoped his brother followed the order.

His lungs searched for more air. He took a small sip, trying to conserve whatever was left. His head spun. His hand collided with...the rabbit cage. The rabbit jumped in circles in the little space. The teacher had said the cage was by the door.

"You may have saved both our asses." Phoenix shoved the cage under his arm and continued the search for escape.

He followed the change in the floor pattern. He had maybe a minute before he would want to rip his mask off. The oxygen tank's alarm rattled his brain. He stayed on his knees and struggled to find the hose and his way out.

He waited for his lungs to burn. Instead, his hand gripped salvation. *The hose.* He nearly sobbed. With the rabbit under his arm, he hurried along the line.

He slammed into a solid mass. The tank emptied.

"Asshole." Hawk's rough hands dug into his arms.

A sarcastic response tripped across his brain. He wasn't sure if he said it. He might be dead.

CHAPTER TWO

*M*ack Scirocco checked the time on her phone again. Late. Of course, she was late. She could waste time looking up the phone number of the Water Course East elementary school she should've saved in her contacts by now, or she could hurry her backside out of the bakery and into her car and be there. The boys wouldn't even notice. At five-years-old, Elliott and Ian were easily distracted with crayons, stuffed animals, or snacks. The after-care teachers would glare at her, whisper behind her back, and judge her as the single mother who always left her twins to be the last ones to be picked up.

Sure, she had forgotten homework assignments or show and tell. Between craft time, music time, and bedtime, she had to cook, clean, pay the bills, and run a business.

Not all parenting came in the same neat box with a fancy bow. Some parents had to work hard to make ends meet and still had a roof over their heads that leaked. She couldn't turn away the last customer who had walked in ten minutes before she closed, asking to see her wedding cake portfolio. Mack's sister, Aria, had sent the bride. Mack needed the money, and she would never let Aria down. Sister's didn't do that kind of thing. The boys were safe at school for an extra fifteen minutes. Okay, twenty-five. Guilt scratched her throat raw when she thought about the relief that washed over her when it hadn't been Water Course East that had burned down.

With a silent promise to be a better person, she snatched her coat from the peg and hurried through the back door that faced the parking lot. Snow fell in a white sheet, covering every flat surface with its cold, wet flakes. The store keys fumbled in her hand while she tried to lock up.

"You bitch." A male voice carried across the lot.

"What the…." She turned to find the culprit cursing at her, but didn't see anyone.

The old, pitted parking lot was dotted with a few cars and a pickup truck. The lot was mostly empty. Typical for the late afternoon in January. If this were the summer, the whole lot would be filled and some people parked illegally. Water Course drew a sizeable tourist crowd from May through September. The extra people were good for her business.

Another quick scan through the screen of snowflakes produced the owner of the voice. Someone with long legs clad in jeans and feet in work boots lay on his stomach under the front end of the truck. The right knee was complete with knee brace and probably getting soaked. Her instincts and the time said get in the car and go.

Water Course might be a safe, sleepy shore town, but crime was everywhere. He could be faking it. Or he was fixing something. But if he was fixing something, wouldn't he be on his back? She shook her head.

"The boys are waiting, Mackenzie," she said. She'd call the police from the safety of her front seat.

"Fuck. Fuck. Fuck." The guy slid out from under the truck and kicked the tire. And cursed again.

At least he wasn't dead, but he did throw his cell phone on the pavement. Recognition landed in her stomach like a good piece of chocolate cake. She should've remembered the legs. She had certainly dragged her gaze over them more than once. But she needed to go. She didn't have time to be a good Samaritan. Or friend.

"Phoenix?" she called out anyway.

Phoenix Egan didn't need her help. He had an entire fire department at his fingertips. Plus, a younger brother who would die for him. But, if Aria found out Mack left her brother-in-law stranded in the snow, she'd never hear the end of it. Assuming he was stranded. Maybe he was just mad at his phone.

"Mack? Wow, am I glad to see you." He strode toward her, favoring his bad leg. The smile never wavered from his handsome face.

The beige wool hat fit his head like it was made for his skull. His flannel shirt flapped open in the wind. The white thermal Henley, streaked with dirt, that lay against his flat stomach must be doing enough to keep him warm, but she couldn't figure out how. Or a man with that much testosterone must run at higher temperatures because Phoenix was all man. Broad shoulders to carry his firefighting gear, and those thick thighs she could wrap her legs around.

Phoenix had a way of being noticed. In her defense, she hadn't had sex in longer than she cared to think about and blamed her raging hormones on noticing his appeal.

She checked her phone. Thirty minutes late. "Do you need to call someone? I saw you throw your phone." If he made it quick, she could lend him hers, but then she'd have to go.

"Yeah, that was stupid. My truck won't start. When I tried to look inside the engine, I dropped the phone, and it broke. Can I bum a lift?"

"I'm late picking up the boys at school. Is there someone you can call? Or a ride service?"

She would like nothing more than to help him. They were practically family with his brother married to her sister, but not today. If her ex-husband found out she was late picking up the boys again, he'd accuse her of being a bad mother. His list of her treasons had grown since she finally mustered up the nerve to leave him. She could never win with David, which was one reason, amongst a list of many, why they weren't married anymore.

The snow continued to cover the area in a white blanket, muffling out any sounds except the faint hint of waves rolling into shore. She loved the winter landscape with its vignette corners made from shortened days. A peaceful quiet settled over them, and for a second she wondered what it would feel like with her head against his chest.

"I don't mind coming along for the ride. You can drop me off home after you grab them. I'm not in a rush."

"Why do you want to do that?" The roads would be slippery and harder to navigate now that she had waited to leave. Everyone seemed to forget how to drive with nothing more than an inch on the ground. The weather would delay her more.

"I haven't seen you in a while. We can catch up."

"You don't want to tell Hawk about your truck." The idea that he wanted to spend time with her warmed her against the ocean breeze coming in and snaking under her clothes, but she knew better. Phoenix had never shown any interest in her other than friendship. The secret fantasizing was all on her end.

"He told me not to buy it. He'll never let me hear the end of it. If I call any of the guys from the firehouse, they'll do the same. I can get it towed, and he'll never know. I need to save a little of my pride." He pointed at his knee. "It's bad enough I fell down the steps of that school and busted it up. Please?" He flashed a toothy grin that made the lines around his dark eyes crinkle.

"Get in. You did a great thing by getting the kids out of the school. I think your buddies from work would give you a little slack on the broken-down truck." Her wipers worked overtime to keep the snow off the windshield as she made her way down Main Street.

"I was just doing my job. It's no big deal."

He never bragged about his work even though he certainly could. He was the complete opposite of her ex-husband who never missed a chance to tell a story about his time in the Army.

"It was a big deal to everyone at that school and their

families. I can't imagine how scared I would be if Elliott and Ian's school caught on fire. You are a hero."

"Not me. My team. My brother. But not me." He picked at his leg brace.

She wanted to reach for him and tell him he didn't have to be humble. Many people were not brave enough to run into a burning building when everyone else ran out, but she gripped the steering wheel instead. He wasn't hers to touch. He wasn't looking for her compliments. Phoenix didn't need her.

She took the turn into the school parking lot like an inexperienced race car driver and bounced in her seat. Hitting the brakes, she parked the car in the no parking zone.

"Stay here. I'll be right back."

"I can come with you." He started to get out of the car.

"Phoenix, it's bad enough I'm late. I'd rather not explain the new man I'm bringing in."

"Is it against the law to have male friends?"

"For some." She shut the door and ran, trying not to slip in the snow.

She didn't like other people knowing her business or jumping to conclusions. If she went inside with Phoenix, someone might think she was out having a good time with a friend. Instead of insuring good customer service so she could keep her bakery going. The bakery was her only source of income.

The empty school hallway echoed with her footsteps. The doors to the multi-purpose room were closed. She heaved a sigh and pulled on one, hoping the teacher hadn't taken the boys somewhere else in the school because she was so late.

The waxed wood floor was dusty and grimy. Blue mats sat piled against the far wall. A set of bleachers had been stretched out, but no one waited there. The stage was empty except for the forgotten music stands pushed to the side. Forgotten like her children appeared to be.

"Shit." She muttered and checked her phone. She may have missed a text or an email about where they waited for her. Nothing indicated after-care would be anywhere else in the building.

Now she'd have to comb the school looking for them. Next time she'd tell the customer they'd have to come back during regular hours. If she had left on time, she would've missed Phoenix and not delayed her arrival more. But he had asked for her help. She wasn't going to let him down too.

"Mrs. Hubert? I'm surprised to see you here." Mrs. Zaggler pranced across the room sashaying her hips. Her bleached blond hair was cut in a short shag around her face and fell longer in the back, but looked as if a good stiff wind couldn't budge it. Her makeup was picture perfect even at the end of the day. Her smile was warm, but no one could always be that friendly.

"I'm sorry I'm so late. I got hung up at work. Did you bring the boys to another part of the school?"

"I'm a little confused. Your husband picked them up."

"Ex-husband. In fact, I went back to my maiden name so please just call me Mack. Why did David pick them up? I pick them up every day after school. We've told you that's our agreement." She had put that agreement in writing so everyone at the school that mattered would know not to allow the boys to leave with David unless she specifically stated.

David would think nothing of interfering with the routine she carefully constructed by pushing his weight around, making everyone step to his commands. He'd pull the father card as if he were the only father on the planet involved in his children's lives.

"I'm sorry. I didn't know anything about your arrangements. When you didn't show up, we tried to reach you at your place of business, but you didn't answer. That's when we called Mr. Hubert."

"You're supposed to call my cell. Always my cell. Not my bakery." She pulled the phone from her pocket and waved it in the air. The school must've called while she was talking to Phoenix. If only she had left the bakery sooner.

The blush on Mrs. Zaggler's cheeks brightened. Mack had specifically filled out every form underlining the importance of calling the cell. Her phone was always on her. If she had to run an errand during the day, she didn't want to miss a call to avoid something like this happening.

"I do apologize for the inconvenience of making you drive over here after your husband picked them up."

"Still my ex-husband. We are divorced, Mrs. Zaggler. I know this is only elementary school, but you must know the meaning of an ex-husband. What time did he come?"

"There's no need to get snippy. It was an honest mistake. It's not as if they went home with a stranger. It's lovely their father is so involved. We're lucky to have someone like Mr. Hubert on our town council."

Mack called on every ounce of strength she had not to begin an argument. No one, except her sisters, knew the truth about David. He had never been lovely or involved. The town would be far luckier if he packed up and left.

"What time did he come for them?" She needed to try and guess where they would go. He'd keep them until past their bedtime without so much as a phone call to her the entire night.

"Right at five."

"You didn't try to call me at all." Her blood burned like scorched milk and sugar. "He showed up, and you let them go. He told you I was running late. Isn't that it?"

"Well, yes, but you do run late so often. I didn't have any reason to believe today was any different."

"Thank you for your help." Which was no help at all. She stormed out of the school and back into the snow.

She would call David and lay into him. He had to stop showing up when it wasn't his day and swiping the kids. If he didn't stick to the custody agreement, she'd have to hire a lawyer again. She couldn't afford to do that, but she would hire one anyway.

Phoenix wiped the snow from her car. She stopped in her tracks as he reached across the hood with the plastic snow brush. His flannel shirt fluttered open. His back muscles flexed under his white Henley as he stretched. She sucked in a breath.

The small, kind gesture brought tears to her eyes. She swatted away her foolish emotions, but it had been ages since a man in her life thought of someone other than himself. He was probably just bored or felt guilty for needing the ride.

Her shaking fingers located David's number in her favorites list, that was irony, and hit the button. David's phone rang and rang then went to voicemail. She bit back a curse.

"David, where are you and the boys? Why did you pick them up without consulting with me first? You know the agreement, and you're forcing me to take you back to court."

Anger shook her voice. She took a deep breath, trying to hold it together because David could be anywhere with her boys. He had the means and the resources. She tried again, and the call returned to voicemail.

"I don't want to fight with you," she began to leave another message. "Just bring them home by eight. Keep an eye on the weather in case it really starts sticking. I don't want them on the road in a storm. And call me." She ended the call and closed the distance to Phoenix.

"Everything okay?" Phoenix shook off the brush before returning it to the trunk.

"I don't know. David took the boys but didn't tell me. Thanks for doing that. You didn't have to. I would've done it."

"No thanks necessary. I wanted to do it. I'm sure the boys are fine and having a lot of fun with their dad. He probably forgot to call is all."

She wanted to believe him. Needed to believe him, because the alternative shook her to her core. "Yeah, you're probably right. I should get you home before the snow gets any worse."

"Hey, I know you're trying to convince yourself you have nothing to worry about because you're locking your jaw like you do, but the boys are fine." He squeezed her arm.

She wanted to lean into him but straightened her shoulders instead. The boys were fine because that's what she needed him and everyone to believe. No one would understand what David was really like. He had everyone convinced he was the perfect husband and father. He knew how to hide the bruises.

Her sisters had figured him out and believed her. They had stuck by her in the divorce, determined to get her free. She didn't want pitying looks or whispers behind her back that said Mack had screwed up again by marrying an abusive man like her father.

"You must be freezing. Let's go." She slipped away from his grip and slid into the driver's seat.

He filled up the space beside her with his long, solid legs and his earthy, male scent. He adjusted his right leg before settling enough to click the seatbelt. She kept her eyes on the road and wished David would at least call her.

"Do you want to grab some dinner?" Phoenix's question dragged her gaze to his.

"No."

"Okay." He held his hands up in surrender while his eyebrows climbed up into his hairline.

"I mean I don't think so, but thanks. I want to be home when David gets there. And it's been a really long day. Maybe some other time?" Snapping at him wasn't going to solve any of her problems. He sat in the wrong place at the wrong time was all.

"Sure." He turned to look out the window. He was shutting her out.

She had disappointed him, but spending time in his company and trying to remind herself they were just friends was too much after the scare she just had. The day had taken its toll. Her back ached from standing all day. Her head pounded from the adrenaline rush at the school. She might even try to take advantage of the few hours of quiet before the boys came back and have herself a glass of wine and a hot bath. She glanced at Phoenix. No, she would not proposition him. She really was pathetic.

She pulled up to his house and put the car in park. The snow came down in fat flakes and covered his sidewalk and grass.

"Are you going to be okay going up to the door with that knee and in this weather? Do you need a cane or something?"

"I'm a big boy, Mack. I think I can handle it. Thanks for the ride." He stumbled and sputtered to get out of the car with one good leg.

"Let me help you." She reached for the driver's door.

"Nope. I got it. Stay put." His words were delivered on a harsh tone.

"I'm sorry. I didn't mean to snap at your dinner invitation." Her heart ached from her bad behavior. She was a lousy friend and should've known the last thing he would want was her help.

"You never mean to snap, but you do." His words bit her skin like a hot cookie tray. He righted himself and adjusted his brace.

"Phoenix, wait." She needed to make this right.

He dropped down and leaned against his arm to look inside the car. "I get it. You're a single working mom who doesn't have time to date. Hawk tried to warn me. Good night, Mack. Drive safely." He closed the door.

What just happened? She stared at the steering wheel a second. He was asking her out on a date? Did she fall on her head? Had he?

She fought the door to get out and slipped on the snow before getting her feet on solid ground. He hobbled up the porch steps, using the railing for balance.

"Phoenix, please hang on a second."

He turned. His jaw was set, and he glared at her with narrowed eyes.

She climbed one extra step to be able to take away his height advantage. "Did you say *date*?"

"What if I did?" He crossed his arms over his chest. A quick smile tugged at the corner of his mouth, but it dropped off before she could be sure.

"You want to go out on a date with me?" The idea melted her insides a little. She had fantasized about this moment for months but never believed it would happen. She certainly wasn't going to be the one to make a move. Her pride had been bruised enough from her marriage. She had been ready to swear off men if necessary, but Phoenix always had her wondering what if.

"What if I do want to sit opposite you at a small table in a dark restaurant and watch you sip wine in that black dress you have?"

"Why?" *He knew she had a black dress?*

Watching him from afar had been safe, especially after things with David started going bad. And Phoenix was always off-limits because he was Hawk's brother. A ridiculous code she had created for herself to protect any sign of vulnerability leaking off her like the smell of rotten eggs.

"Why?" The smile returned and stayed in place. "Because ever since you borrowed my shirt, I can't stop thinking about you."

"That was months ago."

"Nine to be exact."

They had been at Hawk and Aria's. Mack had gone outside to get some air. Her other two sisters had been there. Plus, her two boys, Phoenix, and a couple of guys from the firehouse. The room had closed in on her while she had watched Phoenix laugh and joke around. He had been so confident. So sure of himself. Her boys loved him. He had followed her and placed his sweatshirt around her shoulders to keep the cool spring chill away. But she had been anything but cold.

"Listen, Mack, it's okay if you don't want to go out. I won't ask again. If you don't mind, though, I'd like to go inside. This cold is making my knee hurt. Say hi to the boys for me."

"No."

"No?"

She shook her head and tried again. "I mean yes. I'd like to go to dinner with you. If the offer still stands."

He placed a calloused hand on her cheek. Her heart picked up speed, and her mouth dried out. His lips brushed against hers. They were cold and soft. Her eyes fluttered closed, but she really wanted to watch him in case this wasn't happening. He kissed her for a moment more, and eased away.

"Can you get a babysitter for tomorrow night?" His thumb caressed her chin.

"I think so." She'd ask Aria first. If not, maybe Maggie from the bakery. Or her neighbor. She'd figure it out. She wasn't passing this up.

"Great. I'll see you around six." He kissed her once more, soft and quick.

She floated to her car and all the way home. She had had no idea he liked her that way. She had always thought he was just being nice or friendly. Her radar and her flirting skills were rusted and outdated. She didn't completely trust herself to know when a man even noticed her. She had allowed David to make her doubt herself.

She pulled into the driveway and grabbed the mail. A large manila envelope was shoved in the mailbox. The return address was from David's lawyer's office.

"Oh, no, no, no."

She hurried inside and flipped on the lights. She didn't bother to take off her coat, but ripped through the top of the envelope instead.

Her hands shook as she read the papers. She blinked to make the words come into focus.

David wanted full custody of their twins.

He cited she was incompetent to raise them.

Because she was crazy.

CHAPTER THREE

*M*ack called her lawyer's office. Even though office hours had ended, the sound of a voicemail picking up turned her blood to ice. She left a frantic message that she had to see Virginia. Going through the divorce nearly bankrupted her. Having to hire Virginia Westaway a second time might be the end of her. But she'd find a way.

She ripped off her coat and dialed David again. The call went to voicemail.

"David, I got your little surprise. That's why you grabbed the boys today so you could really put the screws to me. I promise you this; you won't get away with it. It will be a cold day in hell before you take my boys from me. Do you hear me clear enough?" She ended the call and slammed the phone on the table.

She wanted to go get the boys. She should go get the boys. She should march right up the steps to his obnoxious, oversized Victorian on the beach and take her boys back. He had no right to accuse her of being off her rocker. He wouldn't get away with this. He was just lying again.

She scooped up her keys, and her phone rang. David's number flashed on the screen. She had to swipe three times before the call connected.

"David, what the hell are you doing?"

"Now calm down. I didn't know the papers were coming today. I picked up the boys because you were late. The school called me. One had nothing to do with the other."

"Where are the boys?"

"They're asleep. They both had good days at school. We had pancakes for dinner. I checked their backpacks. I'll have them to school in the morning. See? Everything's fine." His voice roughed up her nerves.

"Don't patronize me. The school said you just showed up." She wasn't going to allow him to twist what she said this time.

"Mack, why would I do that? Today is your day with Elliott and Ian. I only showed up because the school called, and I was concerned."

"Why didn't you call me first?"

"I did. You didn't answer."

She hadn't received any calls from David, but to make sure, she put the call on speaker and checked her recent calls. His name wasn't there.

"You didn't call me today."

"I most certainly did. Why would I make that up?"

"Your call isn't in my phone. You didn't call me."

"Mack, technology is so unreliable. I called the bakery's line when you didn't pick up your cell. No one answered at the store. What choice did I have but to get the boys?"

"You could've waited for me to show up." She scratched her head, trying to remember if she heard the phone before she left the bakery. Since she had been with a customer, she could've ignored an incoming call on the bakery line. It was her cell she always answered.

"The boys were glad to see me. I didn't think you'd mind."

"Well, I do mind. You're trying to steal my boys from me." Which was the most important part of this call. He wasn't going to get away with this or pretend as if they were friends having a civil conversation over the weather.

"I don't want to take your visitation away. I just want them to live with me full time. It's what's best for them. You can't be relied on."

"They will never live with you full time. You're out of your mind, you know that? You can't accuse me of being incompetent just because you feel like it. You can't make up lies." But he had made up things while they were married to confuse her or let her believe she was worthless without him.

He let out a long breath. "My lawyer told me not to discuss this with you, but you should know. I have plenty of proof. Today only adds to my case. You neglect our children, Mackenzie. I can't allow that any longer. You live in a hovel. You work crazy hours. Your place of business isn't safe. You allow them to mingle with an alcoholic. And then, of course, there's your past and your past use of drugs."

Her hands clenched into fists. Sweat broke out over

her entire body. The roaring in her ears made forming words difficult. Her home might be small, but it was clean. Her hours were a little unusual, but she had it covered. She never left the boys alone. Her drug use was the anti-depressants she went on after the twins were born, and the alcoholic was her brother-in-law who had been sober for three years now. She trusted her children with Hawk more than her ex.

"I'm coming for my children right now." There was no point in addressing his ridiculous claims. All of them were untrue.

"I can't stop you from doing what you want. You always do. But I don't think it's wise to drag them from their warm beds just to spite me. Why would you want to harm your children further?" His contemptuous tone oozed across the line and turned her stomach.

She bit her tongue against the profanity ready to spill over her lips. He was playing her guilt. He knew she'd back off because she wouldn't want to upset the boys.

"I have every right to come and get my children." She was going just to spite David. He couldn't tell her what to do with her children. If she wanted them home with her, then that's where they should be.

"For now, but let me tell you this, I have recorded our conversation and will make sure to tell my lawyer that you insisted on upsetting our children. Did you know Elliott told his teacher that you slam the phone down after speaking with me and it scares him?"

She hadn't done that. Had she? She had made sure the boys weren't around when she lost her temper. She had kept her anger tamped down while she lived with David, but after she left him, it was as if a faucet had been opened. Her anger spilled in many places, but not in front of her children.

"You're making that up."

"Are you calling our son a liar?"

"He's five. He doesn't exactly have every moment memorized."

"Mackenzie, I'm tired of this conversation. Shall I expect you to come for the children?"

She wasn't sure how to play this. She needed to stay a step ahead of David, but didn't know where that step was. She didn't want to give him any more ammunition even if he was making stuff up.

The custody papers were littered across the kitchen table. She could lose, and she would never survive that. The fight simmered down. She would need to pick the right time to battle him. Now wasn't it, but the idea of leaving the boys at his house still made her chest feel as if someone had stabbed a knife through it.

"Make sure they're at school on time tomorrow morning. I'll be there when you drop them off, and if you aren't, you'll be hearing from my lawyer too." She hung up so she could have the last word.

Hopefully, it didn't backfire.

THE TOWN WANTED to hold a parade in his honor. Phoenix pounded the steering wheel with his fist. Hawk's voice still rung in his ears. His brother had called with the news.

Phoenix drove through town, trying to find a way out

of this. He was only doing his job. Just like everyone else on the crew. He had only gone into the school first because they were down a man, and it was his job to develop an action plan. Any one of them would have found that classroom of kids and brought them out. He wasn't a hero because he went back in for that rabbit. He had been stupid enough to get disoriented. If he hadn't fallen down the steps holding that damn bunny, they wouldn't even have noticed him. Except for Hawk. Hawk noticed everything. It would only be a matter of time before Hawk figured out he suffered from anxiety.

He turned onto Main Street and grabbed the first open parking spot. The mayor was out of his mind wanting this parade. Phoenix only knew one person who could make this go away. The chief's number was up on his new phone screen and dialing before he could change his mind.

"Chief Wylie."

"Chief, it's Phoenix. Can you stop that parade?"

"I wish I could. The last thing I have time for is a parade that will occupy my trucks because one of my boys did what the town pays him to do. But the mayor wants it. Thinks it will be good for the relations with the residents. He's using it to promote the police department and the public works guys."

"I'm not going."

"The hell you aren't. You're the damn guest of honor. He's going to give you a key to the town."

"Please tell me you're yanking my balls." A key to the town? Hawk hadn't mentioned that one.

This parade could not happen because no one knew he

didn't want to go back to work. At least not now. He still hadn't told anyone he panicked when his tank was minutes from running out. If he hadn't tripped over that damn cage, he'd be dead.

"I'm not touching your junk, young man, but I am serious. This is all your fault. If I had come out of that school holding the animal, no one would've taken photos of my old face and bones. But you. You the papers and the news can't get enough of. You need to stop smiling all the damn time. No one is that happy. I'm hiring a guy with no teeth to replace you."

"Have you found my replacement?" His stomach tightened. It would be better if someone took his spot for a while. He had to pull his shit together somehow without anyone catching on to his problem.

"Just a temporary replacement until that knee is better, and you can climb ladders again. Hurry the hell up about it too. I might have to promote Merle soon. He's as old and ugly as I am. I've got to run. The next applicant is pacing outside my damn door." The chief hung up.

He wouldn't be rushing to any fires at the moment. He didn't want to let his guys down. He couldn't go to work until he knew he could trust himself, if he ever could again. Sweat slicked his skin, and his breathing picked up speed. He was a damn mess if he couldn't even think about work without losing his shit.

"Oh, for fuck's sake." He shoved out of the truck into the brisk afternoon.

The cold ocean breeze bit his clammy skin. He drank in the air, trying to make his heart slow. What the hell was wrong with him? He'd never been afraid of anything before. He hadn't even freaked out when Wyatt had died on the job.

Hawk had been the one to fall apart, but he had held it together. He had been the rock Hawk needed. Now he couldn't go five feet without wanting to vomit.

He headed up the sidewalk for his reason to be on Main Street in the first place. Warm and Sticky came into focus like a buoy on a dark night. He smiled, thought of what the chief just said, and clamped his mouth shut. He opened the glass door and inhaled the smell of sugar and vanilla. His breath finally slowed. He needed to see her.

Mack's touch was everywhere. A white counter extended away from the bakery cases, inviting people to sit at it. Stools with distressed tops said customers should stay awhile and drink coffee with their pastries. She had placed a few tables of two made with the same white and light-colored wood off to the side. The floors were textured hardwood and worn, but clean and cared for. Behind the bakery cases were long glass shelves that boasted large menus, mugs, and plates.

The swinging doors leading into the kitchen area opened. Mack wiped her hands on her apron as she came through. Her dark hair was pulled away from her face. Flour coated her red sweatshirt. She smiled when their gazes met, but her eyes said something else. Her lids were heavy, and dark circles made the rest of her skin pale. She was still beautiful enough to steal his breath.

"Hi, Phoenix. What can I get you?" She pulled a to-go cup from the tall pile and held it up.

"Coffee would be great. It's quiet today." He had expected to see customers other than him. Mack's place was popular with the residents and even more so during tourist season.

"The morning rush usually slows down by ten this time of year. Everyone has to get to work." She poured coffee into the to-go cup right to the top.

Heat ran to his core because of her small gesture. She knew how he took his coffee. *Dumb ass.* "And one of those chocolate things I like."

"The éclair? For breakfast?" Her smile broke wide, and she shook her head.

"It's already been one of those days." He slid onto a stool. Coming into the bakery was quickly making his day better. "But I'm looking forward to tonight."

"What's tonight?" She tucked a hair that spilled out of her ponytail behind her ear.

He hesitated. She was joking. Or she wasn't. All he had been thinking about until he got the call about the parade was their date tonight. He kind of hoped she was too.

"I thought we had plans." He sipped the coffee but kept his gaze on hers.

She smacked her head. "I'm sorry. I forgot. Can we reschedule?" She turned away and busied herself with pastry boxes.

"Is something wrong?" He wanted to know what had her looking as if she'd been up all night. Had she been trying to think of a way to let him down?

She put the chocolate in front of him. "I'm fine."

"You don't look fine."

"Thanks, Phoenix. You really know how to sweep a girl off her feet." She dusted her words with a small laugh.

"I'm sorry." Not his smoothest move. "Why are you

canceling? Is it babysitting? I know Hawk and Aria are home tonight. I'm sure they'll watch the boys."

Her lips pressed into a thin white line. "I just can't tonight. Something's come up. I really am sorry."

He should tread lightly around her. If he pushed too hard, she'd only run. It was why he had waited almost nine months to ask her on an official date. Every time he had tried to approach the subject, she sent signals she wasn't interested in anything more than their friendship.

"Maybe I can help. I'm pretty good at solving problems."

"Thanks, but you can't help. I need to be home for my boys tonight. And I need to bring more customers into this bakery before the summer season hits. I just don't have time to get involved."

He had come into the bakery because he needed the sound of her voice and the smile on her face to calm what was bothering him, but she was the one who needed something.

"Mack, take me up on my offer for dinner tonight. You could probably use the night off to forget your troubles for a few hours. I could use it too." He could blame his problems on his leg. She would never have to know his real reasons for wanting to check out for a few hours with the company of a beautiful, smart woman.

He bit into the éclair. Custard dripped down his chin. She laughed at the mess he made. Her laughter eased the knots in his shoulders better than the sugar had. He could listen to her laugh all day long.

"Here." She wiped his face with a napkin. He had to

fight to not grab her and yank her over the counter to kiss her. That would get him a slap across the face.

Her fingers lingered on his skin where the napkin had been. Or so he imagined. She grabbed a towel and wiped the counter.

"Phoenix, don't waste your time with me."

"I'm only asking for one dinner. We've had dinner together before."

"Never alone."

"We're friends. You can have dinner with your friend and tell that friend what's really going on."

She heaved a heavy sigh over her lips and twisted the rag she'd been wiping with. "Why are you such a nice guy?"

"It's a curse." She was giving him the brushoff for sure, but he wasn't going to quit that easily. She had said yes to his invitation not twenty-fours before. Something had changed her mind. He wanted to know what happened.

"Is that why you've never been married?" She changed the subject from herself like a pro. She poured herself a cup of coffee and leaned against the counter.

"Never met the right woman. But we're not talking about me. We were talking about dinner. Not a marriage proposal."

She eyed him over the rim of her coffee mug. The bell over the door chimed. Two women walked in and placed orders. He drank his coffee and finished off his chocolate treat from the sidelines and watched as Mack made her customers feel at home.

When the women finally left, she took the stool beside

him and held his gaze. He wrapped his hands around the cup to keep from touching her.

"Not that you would understand, because you've never been married and all, but my ex-husband is at it again. I need to hire my lawyer, and I don't have the money."

"What's he up to?" He wanted to help her. Hawk had told him her marriage had ended badly, but never gave details. He hadn't asked because if Mack wanted him to know she would say.

"His usual greasy tricks."

"How can I help you?"

"You can't." She shook her head.

"Can you take out a loan to hire the lawyer?"

"I can take out a home equity loan, but I need to fix up a few things first. Which I don't have the money for either. I don't own this building, so I can't borrow against that. I'm pretty much screwed and don't know what I'm going to do." Tears filled her eyes.

Her eyebrows climbed into her hairline, and her hand covered her mouth. She swatted at her face and jumped off the stool. She found a spot behind the counter and started playing with the boxes again.

He hopped off the stool too. His knee complained, but he bit back the curse. He hobbled around the bakery case to her. His approach wasn't his most sure-footed or masculine, but he had to get to her.

"Hey." He squeezed her shoulder. "You'll figure something out. You're smart."

She wiggled out of his grasp and put space between them. "I can't do this right now. I'm really sorry. I like you, but David is fucking up my life. I have to concentrate on keeping my children. I don't have time for any kind of relationship."

"What do you mean *keeping* your kids? Is he trying to take them from you?" Now things were starting to make a little more sense.

She nodded. The tears that threatened before spilled down her cheeks. She wiped them away. "Damn it. I don't want to cry."

"Please let me help you." His instincts were to go find David and beat the crap out of him for making her cry, but he wanted her to see he wasn't like that. He wanted her to come to him for help on her own.

"Like I said, you can't. I wish you could. I need to get the money to hire my lawyer back. I have to fight David. Unless you know how to rob a bank, I'm at a loss." She poured her coffee down the sink drain.

"Hire me." He should've thought of that sooner.

"Excuse me?"

"You said you needed work done to the house. I can fix it up for you, then you can get your loan. I have extra time right now. I just finished a big porch job before I fell. My schedule is clear. I'd be happy to help." He took a few steps back to give her some space to consider his offer.

"I can't afford you."

"Friend's discount." He tried the smile the chief told him to stop using.

"If I pay you, then I won't have the money for the retainer."

"I can lend you money." He reached for his wallet.

"Oh no. That's never happening. I will not borrow

money from you. And it doesn't make sense if I'm going to pay you to work for me."

"I think we're going around in circles here. Hire me so you can get the loan. If you need money up front to retain your lawyer, I'll lend it to you. The second you get the loan approved, pay me back. It's not a big deal." He left his wallet in his pocket.

"It is a big deal to me. I don't want to be indebted to you and then I don't want you to think I owe you. We could never go on a date after all of this." She fisted her hands on her hips and set her jaw.

He was going to lose this argument. He really wanted to help her. He didn't give a damn about the money. She would never hire him for free which is why he offered up the discount. He guessed wrong about the loan part.

"Then just hire me to do the work. I have too much time on my hands right now. You'd be helping me. I'm going crazy hanging around doing nothing."

"What about your knee? How are you going to work with that?"

"Let me worry about that." His knee didn't always hurt. He could probably take the brace off, but he didn't want to tip off anyone just yet he was healing.

He needed to get his head on straight about fighting fires. Working for Mack would distract him long enough to get well again. His knee would heal up completely, and so would his mind. No one would have to know he had panicked. He could save face with his department and help a friend. Because it looked as if that was all she would be at the moment.

"I'll hire you then. But no loan." She pointed a finger at him.

"Fine. But the offer still stands."

She didn't want his charity, and he didn't blame her for her pride. He'd be mad as hell if the tables were reversed.

"No loan, Phoenix. I still want that date someday." A red blush crept up her cheeks.

Maybe he wasn't out of the running just yet. He could talk to Hawk and explain the situation. He would give the money to Hawk and he could offer Mack the loan. She would take a loan from Hawk. Possibly. If she found out what he did, she'd be pissed. He could forget about a date with her.

Or anything else.

CHAPTER FOUR

*M*ack smoothed her black skirt with sweaty hands. Virginia Westaway's mouth moved, but Mack wasn't sure if she heard the lawyer correctly over the roaring in her ears. She should've asked Aria to come with her to translate what jumbled up in Mack's head.

"He has a case? I don't understand." The office with its windows behind Virginia's head tipped on its side. Mack grabbed the edge of the mahogany desk to avoid falling out of the tufted chair. David could not take her boys. She had to fix this.

"I'm saying he's making a compelling argument." Virginia folded her long elegant fingers on the desk. The scarf flowed around her neck and matched the green sweater that looked designer.

Mack wished she could focus on something other than her lawyer's fashion sense. Which Virginia had in spades. She probably had on a pair of unique but stunning shoes too. That wasn't the reason Mack had hired her. Virginia was known for her tactics in divorces and custody battles. She cost a fortune, but she was worth it. David had been unwilling to give over a lump sum of money. Virginia had fought for the down payment on the house Mack needed. She hadn't wanted any money from David, but Virginia also convinced her to take what was rightfully her.

"Is this because he doesn't want to pay child support anymore?" She shouldn't be surprised by what David was doing, yet she was.

Her divorce had not been amicable. David had tried to stop her with threats several times. She had stayed for the boys. But when he had put his hands on her that one time, it was enough. She had grown up in a house with an abusive father. She didn't want to be that woman anymore. Her sisters had helped her leave.

"I don't know what his motivations are. If he gets full custody, he won't have to pay you anything, but raising two children full-time is far more expensive than writing a check each month. Kids always need or want something." Virginia handed her a tissue.

"He can't do this." She blotted her eyes. She hadn't even noticed they were leaking.

"He's doing it. My advice is to fight fire with fire. You're going to have to go after his character as well."

"But what he said about me isn't true."

"Have you taken antidepressants during your married life?" Virginia went over to a small refrigerator tucked in the corner of the room and removed two water bottles. Her high-heeled shoes with intricate details on the front made Mack's bank account groan. She handed one to Mack. "Sorry this isn't vodka."

"I took antidepressants for a short period, but I'm not crazy." The medicine had been temporary. She had needed some help getting over the blues. David had kept her alone most of the time with two infants. He would never tell her when he was coming back, saying he had business.

When she would get mad about having to juggle the boys alone for ten or twelve hours a day without help, he would tell her she had misunderstood. That he had helped often, and he didn't want her bothering Aria with their marital issues. He said it was no one's business.

"We know you aren't crazy. That isn't the point. His lawyer is going to use that against you. Plain and simple. How about the number of times you're late picking up the boys from school?"

"Sure, I've been late, but—"

Virginia put up a hand. "No buts. It will be a yes or no question. You left the boys at school waiting for you just the other day. Have you ever forgotten them somewhere?"

"He wouldn't." Her breath caught. He knew that was an accident.

"He did. It's in the complaint." She tapped the papers.

It had been only once. She had gone to the beach with Aria and Hawk and the boys. She thought Aria had the boys. Aria thought she had them. But Elliott and Ian had wandered off looking for the ice cream man with the balloons. It took over an hour to find them sitting on a beach towel licking cones with Maggie from work. Maggie had said she called, but Mack had left her phone on the beach towel while she ran up and down the sand frantically. She hadn't planned on telling David anything, but Ian had ratted her out in that five-year-old way.

"What am I going to do?"

"You need to find a way to fight back. It isn't going to be easy. He's a decorated war hero. He's successful. Pays his taxes and child support. On paper he's a good father. What would the boys say about living with him?"

"They're five. They want to go wherever they don't have to take a bath."

"They won't have a final say, but the judge will ask them. I suggest you get yourself in order. Clean out your medicine cabinet. Don't drink. Don't get into any fights. Don't be late. Dot all your i's. We'll submit a countersuit for full custody."

"Can I lose this?"

"Can anyone confirm the things he's saying? Has anyone seen you out of control in public? What about relationships with other men? Have you brought strangers home?"

"What kind of a person do you think I am?"

"Mack, this isn't about what I think. This is about the picture David paints." Virginia dropped back down into her chair.

"I only dated one man since the divorce. A couple of dates." She hadn't really liked him. It had been a couple of nights after Phoenix gave her his shirt. She had thought about Phoenix the whole time.

"Did you bring this guy home?"

"Shit. This is awful. It was one damn night. David came back with the boys early. They were supposed to spend the night with him, but Elliott wanted to come home. That's what David said anyway." She had been surprised by their unexpected return. It wasn't like Elliott to give up a chance to sleep at David's. Had David known she'd brought a man back to the house? He had followed her before, but she had never told anyone.

"Oh, boy. Okay. Put on your nun habit for now. No dating."

She swallowed the lump in her throat. Now was probably a bad time to mention the hot firefighter coming to her house later. But Phoenix didn't count. The boys knew him. He was practically an uncle to them.

"What next?"

"If you know anything that can tarnish David's reputation, find it. I'm not afraid to use it."

"There isn't anything. And I won't make it up. I can't be like him." She should have kept a journal while they were married. Something to document who he really was.

"Think on it, okay? In the meantime, I file a counter-suit. We wait for a hearing date. Probably a few weeks or a month. I'll try to push it out, but the other side will fight me. In the meantime, keep to your regular schedule. The custody stays the same. Don't be late picking up the boys. Don't leave them anywhere. Try not to leave them with anyone other than your sister. Go to work and come home. Put a lid on your social life for the next month."

"What about Hawk's drinking problem? David brought that up." She couldn't tell Aria the boys couldn't stay with her through this. That would kill them both.

"Is he drinking now?"

"Sober three years. Goes to work. He runs a grief

retreat with his brother for firefighters who lost a family member in the line of duty."

"I wouldn't worry about what David tries to say about him. Your sister and brother-in-law are good people. His firefighter angle works in his favor."

She let out a long breath. She could continue to be friends with Phoenix. Just no dating. She would have to stick to that until this was all over.

"I'll show you out. My assistant will take your payment. I'll try to get David to pay my fees as well. We'll see." Virginia came around the desk.

"Thanks for everything." She held out a hand, but Virginia folded her into a hug.

She wanted to hang out in Virginia's embrace until she thought she could face what was in front of her, but that would be inappropriate. Mack patted her back instead and eased away.

"You're going to be fine."

She could only manage a nod. The hug threw her off-balance. Other than her sisters, she didn't have a female in her life she could look up to. It had been Pop she went to when things at home were tough, which they always were with her father. It hadn't been easy to be the second oldest of four girls with no mother around.

She made her way to the front of the building on shaky legs. This whole event was more like falling off a tight rope with no net below. Virginia wasn't even some kind of safety device, but Virginia knew what she was doing, and everything would work out. She had to keep believing that.

"Can I leave my deposit?" she said to Rich working behind the reception desk.

"Of course. How would you like to pay?" He turned away from his computer and stuck out his hand.

"Can I give you a check?" She had taken a cash advance on her credit card. She was maxed out now. Without that home equity loan, she was screwed. If she couldn't make her mortgage payment, David would have something to really hold against her.

"There's a service fee is if it's returned. I say that because the last three people who paid us with checks had them bounce. I'm sorry. I know yours won't, but Virginia wants me to mention it from now on." Rich rolled his eyes as if they were conspirators in a drama.

"It won't bounce."

She might not have any money for food after this, but who needed to eat?

MACK'S STOMACH growled as she pulled into the school parking lot five minutes ahead of schedule. She'd head straight home from here, make a quick snack for her and the boys, before Phoenix arrived. He wanted to look at her list of house projects and give her a quote. She wouldn't think about the money. All she really wanted was to hug her boys and inhale their sweet scents. She could panic tomorrow.

She found a parking spot at the back of the lot and headed into the school for the parent pickup line. She would have to stand at the end of that line because the bulldozer mommies would have shown up an hour ago and waited on the sidewalk for the doors to open to them. No matter what, she'd never be here that early. She had a job and no one else to rely on.

The line of mothers snaking around the multi-purpose room wore carbon copies of the fashionable black down coat with their legs swathed in exercise pants of varying colors. Their makeup was perfectly applied for people who dressed as if they'd just rushed from the gym. Some of them were her regular customers, but most of these women preferred the coffee shop chains that offered baked goods prepared on the other side of the country. They either whispered to the mother next to them or they concentrated on their phones.

She took a quick glance at her phone too, but nothing seemed to interest her at the moment. Her mind still raced over her appointment with Virginia and the suggestion of sullying David's reputation. If she had something, anything that would make him look unfit for full custody, she would use it. The problem was she didn't have any kind of concrete proof. She only had her word against his. The bruises had healed.

A cackle of sound burst through a set of doors in the far corner of the room. Voices carried into the rafters. Tinny laughter bounced off the walls. She searched for her two boys, scanning the crowd of elementary school children tumbling over each other as they tried to find a seat on the bleachers.

Elliott hopped into the gym with his blue coat hanging off one shoulder. He dragged his backpack behind him. His hair stuck up in different directions as if he had glue on his hands when he decided to pull at it. His boots were untied. Ian followed close behind. His backpack sat on its rightful place on his back. His coat was on and buttoned to the neck. He stood his full height with his head held high. She hoped David had double-tied his laces because that was how Ian liked them. He pointed to a spot for him and Elliott to sit. He shook his head at something Elliott said. Elliott dropped onto the seat with a thump and a frown.

Her heart squeezed. Her legs begged to be set free so she could run to them. She'd missed them so much, but she had to wait her turn. She hated this line even if it was for safety.

She tried to catch the boys' glances, but they were busy with their friends. She'd pull out some cookies from the freezer when they got home. The last time she'd made Pop's secret chocolate chip recipe she had made extra cookies for a special occasion. This was special enough. She'd even let them have chocolate milk. They'd careen off the walls all night, but it would be worth it.

"Hello, Mrs. Hubert." Mrs. Zaggler, the second-grade teacher, handed over the clipboard for her signature.

"Hello, Mrs. Zaggler. I know we've discussed this before. I don't go by Hubert any longer."

"Not even for your boys?"

Was it too much to ask another woman to understand what she must be going through? Did this teacher have to judge her because she chose to change her name? She clenched her fists and took a deep breath. "We're a modern family. Can you please call over the boys?"

"Mrs. Stone, please send Ian and Elliott."

The boys tumbled over each other on their way to her. Elliott pulled himself together and ran. She scooped him up in her arms. He gripped her around the neck and planted a wet kiss on her cheek.

"Mommy, do you want to see the picture of the dragon I drew?" Elliott unzipped his backpack.

"Sure, buddy. In the car. Let's get Ian and go." She grabbed the bag and draped it over her shoulder, otherwise everything in it would be all over the floor.

Ian had stopped halfway to her. His face crumpled. Her stomach dropped. He took off his backpack and threw it to the ground. Tears fell down his red-stained cheeks. She hurried to him.

"What's the matter? Are you sick?" She placed her hand on his forehead.

He pushed her hand away. "Where's Daddy?"

Her brain took a second to register Ian wasn't complaining about stomach pains or a headache. Or even someone teasing him. "Daddy doesn't come today. I pick you up after school."

"You didn't yesterday. I want Daddy." He pounded her shoulders with tiny fists.

"Mrs. Hubert, please take the boys to the side. I need to get these other children out of here," Mrs. Zaggler said.

She offered a small smile in exchange for an apology and tried to scoop up Ian. He stiffened his body like a surfboard. She struggled with his dead weight and his yelling in her ear for his father.

Elliott tugged on her coat. "Mommy, why is Ian crying?" Not waiting for an answer, he started crying too. The boys were so in tuned with each other they often took on the mood of the other one. The cries echoed off the walls of the large room.

Wearing her coat inside the building turned into a bad idea. Sweat broke out under her arms as she carried Ian in one arm and pulled Elliott with the other. Her high-heels slipped on the waxed wood floor. She almost crashed to the ground in a pile of unhappy children.

"Can I help you?" Mr. Kelly came in from the other door in his crisp white shirt and blue tie.

Great. The principal stared at her as she lost the battle with her children. Mothers stared from their spots around the room and in the line. Someone was probably taking photos. Bile rose in her throat. What if David got wind of this?

"Mrs. Hubert, can I help?" Mr. Kelly took Elliott's hand.

"We're fine. Thank you." She reached for her son, but Elliott pulled away. Traitor.

"Where's my daddy?" Ian screamed again.

"He's not coming." Her insides shook. It took all her energy to keep it together. Of course, it wasn't Ian's fault. He was a child, but she would really like to pop David about now. "I'm sorry. He thought his father was picking him up today."

"No need to apologize." He led the way into the hall. Without the echo of the gym, Ian's cries lowered. "Can I help you get to the car?"

"No, thank you. Ian, please stop crying. You can see Daddy later." Heat burned her cheeks. Other mothers and their children came crashing through the doors into the hall. She avoided the judgmental glares boring into her back. "I really need to be going."

Mr. Kelly smiled and took Elliott by the hand. "I don't mind helping." And headed out the door.

She had no choice but to follow with her hysterical child.

"I'm over there. The Accord." David wouldn't let her keep the minivan after the divorce. The vehicle was in his name. She had to scrounge together enough money to buy the old Honda, or she would've been without a way to get around.

"Let me help you." He eased Ian out of her arms while she unlocked the doors. "Hey, buddy. How about we take a deep breath like we practice in P.E.? Ready?" Mr. Kelly mimicked what he wanted Ian to do.

At first Ian just watched, but a miracle she would never have been able to perform transpired before her eyes. Ian followed along. The cries turned to hiccups. Mr. Kelly buckled Ian in. She ran around the other side to help Elliott with his seat.

"Thank you for that. I don't know why he reacted that way." She closed the car door for a blessed second of peace and tugged at the zipper on her coat.

"Kids always give moms the hardest time. He's probably tired from a long day and still adjusting to the new living arrangements." He loosened his tie and unbuttoned the top button of his shirt. His perfect white teeth formed a vivid smile.

He was tall and well built. His hair was cut close. Word on the playground was he was divorced, no kids, and an avid surfer. Plenty of the single moms had eyes on the principal, who wasn't from Water Course, but had found his way to them from the city. She could admire his good looks. Even his way with cranky children, but her head wasn't turned. She wanted the firefighter she wasn't allowed to date at the moment.

"Those living arrangements have been in place for a year. I thought he'd be used to it by now."

"In good time. You're a wonderful mother."

"How can you tell?" She stole a glance in the car. The boys were sharing a book. The tears seemed to have subsided for now.

"I have a sense about these things. Um, I wasn't sure how to bring this up…"

Oh, boy. He was going to ask her out. She would let him down easy. "Just say it. It's always easier to get to the point."

"Thanks. I appreciate that. I've been asked to answer questions on your character." He shoved his hands in his pockets.

"Excuse me?" The date question would've been better. At least she hadn't tried to spare him the embarrassment of asking by sticking her foot in her mouth. That would have been more embarrassing than her poorly behaved child.

"Your ex-husband's lawyer reached out to the school. They want a character sketch on you. I told them I would not answer anything like that. My instincts are rarely wrong about parents. I know you're invested in your children, but I want to warn you some of the teachers could be asked as well. I can't control what they say in a deposition. I suggest you be careful around here."

Someone had talked. He was trying to warn her. Her big mouth had gotten her in trouble again, and she didn't even know how or when. Not every teacher liked her. She had complained about the boys not being challenged enough and about the new music teacher who couldn't come up with a suitable program for kindergartners. She stifled a groan. She would never learn. David would be able to stack a huge case against her because she never knew when to shut up.

"Mr. Kelly, do you know my ex-husband?"

"I've never met him, but I do know he served our country. Your children seem to love him very much. That's all I need to know."

That was the problem. What everyone knew about David would only paint him as a saint. Her head spun. The only time she ever stayed quiet would be the end of her.

"Thank you again for your help with the boys." She stuck out her hand.

This conversation was over. She wanted to get out of the cold and away from this school and the nice principal who hadn't been looking at her with interest, but pity.

CHAPTER FIVE

*P*hoenix checked his phone again. He must have the wrong time. He was supposed to meet Mack at her house after she picked up the boys from school. She should've been here by now.

The sun dipped below the bare tree-tops, washing the color out of the sky. The wind off the ocean blew around the houses and chilled his skin. The street with its small houses lined up in a neat row sat quiet. The cold weather pushed everyone inside. Lights popped on in scattered rhythms.

Winter at the beach brought a solitude over the town like a fire blanket snuffing out all the sounds except for the ocean. With fewer people around, the fire calls died down some. People didn't tend to build bon fires on the beach they didn't know how to handle in the winter. Or throw too much gasoline on outdoor grills.

He missed his job, but the idea of running into a building and losing his ability to see still made the sweat slick his skin. That wasn't him. Not even all those years under his father's thumb. As the middle kid in the family, it had become his job, along with Wyatt, to stand up against his old man to protect Hawk. His brothers had watched out for him plenty of times too. Hawk had stepped in front of a punch their father threw that was meant for Phoenix. Hawk had crashed into the wall and broke the plaster with his head. Phoenix hated his father but had never feared him. The only thing that ever scared him was when Wyatt died in a fire.

He shook the thoughts away and checked the time again. Maybe he had the wrong day. He heaved the disappointment and his ass off the front porch steps. His knee protested against the pressure he applied without thought. He gripped the railing, readjusted his weight, and tried to stand like a man again.

A champagne-colored Accord turned the corner and headed his way. A smile tugged on his lips. She parked and jumped out of the car.

"I'm sorry we're late. Were you waiting long?" she said on a long breath. Her hair spilled out of her ponytail. She swiped the hair away from her face only to have the wind blow it back. Her cheeks were as red as a fire hydrant, but she was beautiful.

"I just got here. Perfect timing." He limped over and opened the back door. "Hey, buddy. You need help?"

"You're not my dad." Ian stared up at him with wide eyes.

"Nope. But if it's okay with you, I can unbuckle those straps."

"You don't have to," Mack said.

"I want to. It's practice for when Hawk becomes a

dad." He would be an uncle soon, and he was looking forward to it. He liked the idea of Hawk starting a new family for him to be a part of. He even entertained the fantasy, for a minute, of having his own kids someday.

"Ian, make sure to say thank you to Mr. Egan."

"Mr. Egan? Really? Since when?" He didn't understand her sudden cold shoulder.

"I don't know. I want them to be polite and respectful to adults." She assisted Elliott out of his seat.

"Mack, I've been hanging around all of their lives. I don't want to be Mr. Egan."

"Okay. Okay. Mr. Phoenix, then."

"Just Phoenix. Please."

He fumbled a little with the straps. Ian showed him how to do it. A fuzzy warmth filled his chest while the boy put him in his place. "You're smart, Ian."

"Thank you, Mr. Phoenix."

Mack juggled her kids and all their stuff up the front walk and to the porch. Those heels made her calf muscles wink at him with each step. Something stirred in his low belly. She wanted to be just friends. He had to respect that but could admire her from afar. She corralled the kids inside and made them wash up.

"You make that being a mom stuff look easy," he said.

The kitchen was small but neat. The space wasn't used well, but that had more to do with whoever had designed the layout. Mack had made the most of what she had to work with. Pictures drawn by Elliott and Ian decorated the front of the fridge. She kept a grocery list on a chalk-board hanging on the wall.

She laughed and kicked off her shoes. "Yeah, right. I'm

horrible at it. Do you want to see the projects I have in mind?"

"Right down to business."

"It's been a long day. I still have to make the boys dinner and get them in the bath. I just want a glass of wine, to get out of this skirt, and read a good book." She pulled a file from the drawer and laid it open on the counter.

"Go change. I'll have the wine waiting when you get back. You can tell me what you had in mind instead of a tour. I'm not a bad cook. I could help you with dinner too."

Her gaze dropped to the floor then back up to his. "Phoenix, that's too much."

"I'm just trying to be friendly." Maybe his intentions weren't all about friendship, but he wanted to be near her and make her day easier. Being with her made the noise in his head quiet down. He didn't have to think about work or hiding the fear that could give him away in a second.

"I don't want to confuse things." She pushed the file away.

Things were already confused for him. Because he had finally found the nerve to ask her out on a date, he didn't want to go back to just being friends. He wanted to take the jump and see where things went with them. If he didn't try, he'd always be wondering what it would have been like with her.

"Mack, we'll do whatever you want, but please take a risk on me." Because he even though he couldn't take a risk on himself at the moment, he would never hurt her.

"It's not you. It's my situation. David can't find out I'm

seeing someone. He'll try to use it against me. He'll accuse me of being a slut or some other awful thing." She pulled her hair out of the holder and retied it.

"Those things aren't true about you." He wouldn't allow David or anyone to tell lies about her.

"I don't want you to get hurt in the crossfire."

"I'm a big boy. I can handle myself. You worry about the boys. I'll worry about me." He had handled bullies worse than David Hubert. There wasn't anything that David could throw his way that he couldn't block.

"I don't want to lose you as a friend if something goes wrong. I can't handle that too." She pulled the file back and fidgeted with the papers.

"Do you want me to leave right now?" He held his breath. He didn't want to go, but she had to believe she could trust him.

"No." She held his gaze and rewarded him with her smile.

"Losing my friendship won't happen. I'm not going anywhere, but we'll do whatever you want. I just want you to be happy."

"Having you here is one of the best parts of my day today."

Heat rolled over his body. He let his smile spread wide. He still had a chance. "Go get changed. I'll pour the wine, and you can show me what's in that folder."

"I'll be right back. The wine glasses are in the cabinet next to the sink." She hurried off.

He grabbed the glasses and poured the wine. Her acquiescence to have a drink with him resembled a small victory. He'd take it. He wasn't letting her get away too easily, but he'd never push her. Her friendship meant too much to him. He scanned her pages in the folder to see what she had in mind for the house.

Soft, tiny feet padded into the kitchen. "Hello," a squeaky voice said.

He turned. Elliott stared at him with wide eyes like Mack's. Elliott clamped his fist around some Legos and a held a booklet in the other.

"Hey there." He put the wine to the side.

"Are you good at reading? I'm okay, but I don't know all the words in this. Could you help me?" Elliott handed over the booklet.

"I'm okay at reading." He took the book and pointed to the table.

"What happened to your knee?" Elliott climbed onto the chair belly first before plopping down beside him.

"I fell down some stairs."

"Did someone push you?"

"I was clumsy."

"Joey pushed Daphne on the playground. He got a time-out, but she didn't have to wear anything on her leg. Does it hurt?"

"Yes." The rapid questions made the corner of his mouth curl up, but he didn't want Elliott to think he might be laughing at him. The boy with his messy dark hair and wide eyes made him want to smile from deep inside his gut.

"Did you go to the doctor? Mom says when you're hurt you go to the doctor. Mom went to the doctor once. I saw her get hurt. That was when my daddy lived with us.

Do you live with your kids?" Elliott arranged his Legos on the table.

"I don't have kids." He wanted to ask more questions about what Elliott saw, but wasn't sure how to go about it. Mack never talked about her married life. He never pushed but wished he had.

"Why not? You don't like kids?" Elliott scrunched up his face as if that was the craziest idea he had heard.

"I like kids. Hey, Elliott, when Mom got hurt, did you see what happened?" He couldn't stop himself. He had to know.

"I don't think so. She was crying. I cry sometimes too. Mom says that's okay."

"It sure is." That was never the message he and his brothers got. Egan men never cried. He had only cried when Wyatt died.

"My Aunt Aria has a baby in her belly. Did you know that?" Elliott handed him the book.

"I did. Did you know she's married to my brother?" He flipped through some of the colorful pages before going back to the beginning.

"Uncle Hawk is your brother? Wow. Ian is my brother. Are you twins too?" Elliott climbed onto his lap and settled his back against Phoenix's chest. The warmth of his little body seeped through his shirt.

"Hawk is my younger brother by two years." He held the book open for Elliott to see.

"You're the oldest. Ian is older than me. I don't remember by how long, but it was only a little time. Can you read from here?" Elliott flipped through the pages until he found the spot he wanted.

A small gasp made his head snap up. Mack had swapped the skirt for sweatpants and an oversized sweatshirt. Her hair fell in long waves around her shoulders. A smile lit up her face. She hadn't smiled like that in a while. The heat in his chest spread through his body again.

"I didn't mean to take so long. Am I interrupting?" Mack took the chair opposite him.

"The wine is on the counter." He pointed over his head. "Elliott and I were just about to start reading. Do you want to join us?"

She took the book from Elliott's hands and closed it. "Sweetie, could you play in the other room until dinner? I have to talk to Phoenix."

"But he was going to read to me."

"I'll read to you later." She scooped Elliott from his lap and plopped him on his feet.

"But this is a boy book."

"I can handle boy books. Now go." She handed him the book and scooted him from the room.

"Did I do something wrong?" He misread the smile somehow.

"I don't know what I'm doing here. I agreed to have you help me with the house projects, but I come in here and see you with him. My first thought was how nice. You're so good with kids. It's no wonder it was you who saved that classroom full of children. But my next thought is I can't allow you to get close to Elliott and Ian. I can't have them hurt. I can't get hurt anymore."

He wasn't some kind of hero because he saved those kids. Anyone would've done what he did. He wished everyone would just forget about it and let him get on with his life. "I'm not going to hurt you."

"You were being so kind to Elliott just now. That's what he needs. Both boys need a good male role model in their lives."

"David isn't nice to them?" The hairs on the back of his neck stood up. Her comment combined with what Elliott had just said made him want to have a very long conversation with David.

"He is. I think he is at least. I can't prove he isn't. Never mind. Let's just talk about the projects."

"Mack, what's going on with David? Is he dangerous?" He could be overreacting, but in his line of work, he'd seen enough evil to pay attention to the tingle up the back of his neck.

Fire calls were often the need for medical attention. He had pulled couples apart that were ready to kill each other. He had found dead bodies at scenes where the person had been murdered first then set on fire to cover it up.

"No. Of course not. That's silly." She grabbed the wine and held up the folder. "Where should we begin?"

He didn't believe her, but she would have to trust him enough to say something. Or he could ask Aria a few questions. He would not allow David to hurt her or the boys. He'd kill him first.

"Are you sure you want me to stay on the job? I don't want to confuse things for you or the boys." He needed to know where he stood with her.

"I want you." Her eyebrows shot up.

He bit back the retort dying to slip free, but that was his cue.

He ignored the pain in his knee and cleared the space between them. He wanted to be close to her and inhale her sexy, sweet scent. He clasped her chin between his fingers and tilted her head up. He wanted her to be looking right at him when he said this.

"I'm not going to allow your ex-husband to stop what's happening between us. I don't know what this is yet, but I want the chance to find out. If I know anything, it's life's too short. We can go at your pace, but unless you tell me to get the hell out of your house right now, I'm going to kiss you."

MACK SWALLOWED the lump in her throat. Phoenix's fingers on her chin made her skin tingle in a warm, juicy way. His intense gaze held hers and fired up the electric current between them. She had spent months wondering what his mouth would feel like on hers and just as many months wondering when she finally noticed him as a full-blooded male and not just Hawk's brother.

She had a lot at risk here. If David got wind of a relationship with Phoenix, he'd use it against her. But Phoenix was such a good man. He really seemed to like the boys, and they liked him. Why should she be denied some happiness and affection in her time of need? She had earned a chance to enjoy herself after all she'd been through. But if she screwed up even a little, David would take the boys. She couldn't let that happen. And she could never tell Phoenix what David was really like because if he looked at her with pity she would crumble. She wanted Phoenix to keep looking at her as if she were the only person on the planet.

"No one can know." The words escaped on a whisper. Her heart fought against what she just said. She wanted to be all in and shout to the world they were together. That would have to wait.

"You want us to be a secret?" The confusion in his eyes reflected back at her. He moved his hand to her waist.

"I can't let David find out. We can't slip up. Not in front of the boys. If you can live with that arrangement for now, then kiss me. But if you can't, then go. Please."

"I can live with that."

He leaned in and pressed his lips to hers. They were warm and soft. She sank into him and wrapped her arms around his waist. Her palms splayed out on his big, muscular back.

She forgot reason when his tongue pushed open her mouth and sought hers. His kiss was long and deep. The kiss of a man who had perfected this move. For a second, she hesitated. It been so long since she kissed a man. What if he noticed her inabilities? Had David been right about her less than average love making?

He didn't end the kiss but tilted her head back to take it deeper. All the heat in her body traveled south. Phoenix held her against his strong chest while his hands stroked her back. She wanted to cling to him like a life preserver and still drown in the taste of him.

Tinny laughter floated somewhere in the back of her mind. Logic tapped on her shoulder and said, *time to knock it off.* But madness made her want to rip his clothes off.

With regret in her bones, she eased out of the kiss. He smiled down at her with something that looked like pride in his gaze.

"That was nice, but the boys could come in." Her words were hoarse with desire. Nice was an understatement.

He ran his thumb over her chin again. His touch reignited the heat in her core. She wanted to pull him close and feel his lips against hers.

"No problem. We can pick this up when it's a better time. How about you tell me about the projects you want done, and I can help you make dinner."

"What about your fee? I need to know what to budget for." She eased away from him before one of the boys came into the kitchen.

"Pay me later. I don't care about the money." He leaned against the counter and crossed his arms over his broad chest.

"That isn't fair. You're working. You should get paid. I can't accept that kind of charity." She needed to focus her attention somewhere other than his legs. She fumbled in the cabinets for a box of pasta.

"Mack, being with you is what I care about. If you insist that your dignity or your honor is at stake, we can work out the payment later. After the work is done. That's my deal. Take it or leave it." He cocked an eyebrow at her.

"You're too stubborn for your own good." She bit on the inside of her cheek to keep from laughing and encouraging him.

He was always so sure of himself. He had to be to run into a burning building to save strangers. She was attracted to his confidence and his belief everything would work out. Juggling her feelings and this thing that was about to take off between them could prove difficult. She didn't trust herself to take it slowly. She needed boundaries to keep her heart and her life safe.

"Are you agreeing to my terms?"

"There are other contractors who will provide an itemized estimate." But not that sexy smile or those legs she wanted to run her hands over.

"True. But none as good as I am." He leaned in. His lips brushed her ear. "And no one else you'll want to kiss. Think of the benefits of having me at your disposal."

Her heat traveled south again.

"Help me make dinner." She pushed him away.

He tilted his head back and roared with contagious laughter. Together, they managed some pasta with home-made tomato sauce she had in the freezer. He turned a loaf of nearly stale bread into something delicious. He even sautéed up some meatballs for the boys.

The kitchen filled with inviting smells. His presence beside her as they cooked was like a favorite cookie recipe that no longer needed to be tested. He took up so much space with his long, solid legs and wide shoulders. Yet he fit as if he'd planned to be there all along.

After she tucked the boys in, she and Phoenix discussed the projects over another glass of wine. He had built a fire while she read bedtime stories. The living room was warm instead of the usual chill that accompanied the room because she didn't have the energy most nights to bother. The flames provided the only light. A golden glow dressed up the space.

"I'll start tomorrow." He sat on the opposite end of the couch, never allowing his gaze to slip away. His intensity soothed some of the jagged edges of her broken ego.

She wanted to climb over to his side and kiss him again, but she needed to stay put. Many nights Elliott popped out of bed with a request or a remembered something he needed to share. She couldn't take the chance until she was sure they were in for the night. And even then, rushing before thinking could backfire.

"I'll give you the spare key so you can come whenever you want. I drop the boys off at school around seven, then I head into work. I pick them up at four from after care. We'll come straight back here." She finished her wine and put her hand over the glass when he tried to pour more. She needed her wits about her now, but the wine had added a fuzzy feeling to her head. She couldn't take her eyes off his lips.

"Can I ask how you run a bakery but don't get to work until after it opens?" His words held curiosity not contempt. He leaned forward and rested his arms on his thighs, but shifted to accommodate his knee.

"Are you okay? Can I get you some ibuprofen for that?" She admired how he never complained about his injury. If David got a papercut, he would never shut up about it.

"I'm fine. Don't worry about me and this dumb knee."

Her fingers itched to reach out and touch him. She missed the intimacy of innocent touching. Just a graze on the shoulder as she passed by had been lost to her years ago when David became hateful.

"Maggie is an angel in disguise. She gets there about four to open up. Carlos comes in then too and starts baking. Maggie assists him. I make sure everything is ready for them each night before I leave. I'm late so many times picking up the boys because I want the bakery ready when they get there. It's my place and my responsibility."

"You take on a lot by yourself." He tapped her leg with his finger.

"I don't have many people to rely on." The fire made the room too hot. She took off her sweatshirt.

"Do you miss Liv and Blair?"

How wasn't he sweating in that flannel shirt? "Of course I do, but it's at weird times. Like when I'm baking and something goes wrong. I want to tell Liv all about it. I check the time to see where she might be and what she's doing before I send a text because I don't want to bother her. I wish she were still in the same town, but she's never coming back to live here."

She and her three sisters had dealt with the scars of their tortured childhood in very different ways. Liv and Blair put as much space as they could between them and Water Course. Sometimes she wondered if that had been the better idea. Especially now, with her hormones out of control.

"What about Blair?"

"Blair and Aria are closer." There wasn't anything left to say on that matter.

She wanted to ask how often he thought about Wyatt, and if he wished he'd been working that night, but that had never been a topic they discussed. She had learned from Hawk that Wyatt's death was off-limits.

"Have you received your court date?" His deep voice grounded her back on the couch with him only inches away.

"Can we talk about something else? I don't want David creeping into my space right now." The fantasy had taken hold. David was the last person invited.

"We can talk about whatever you want, but how do you plan on stopping him?"

"I have to find a kink in his character. I just don't know where to begin looking. Aren't you hot?" She got up and opened a window.

"I'm fine." He narrowed his eyes. "It's getting late. I should let you get to whatever it is you do once the boys are asleep." Phoenix pushed off the couch but didn't make a move to come any closer.

"Yeah, five a.m. comes around pretty quickly. Thanks for all the help tonight." She stayed by the window.

"Make sure that fire is out before you go to bed. Or I can put it out now, if you want."

She wasn't going to bed any time soon. Not with all the thoughts bouncing around in her head. "I'll take care of it. Thanks."

"Then I'll see you tomorrow."

"Yup. I'll walk you to the door." She hesitated to allow him to go first. She couldn't resist bumping into him.

He grabbed his coat and shrugged into it. His shirt rose up and revealed a piece of his flat stomach and a smattering of black hair dipping into his jeans. She bit the inside of her cheek.

"Sleep well, Mack." He placed a soft kiss on her cheek. A hint of spice caught her off guard.

Her throat closed up, and any chance of a response died on her lips.

He closed the door with a soft click. She leaned against it and hung her head.

She was in over her head.

She should stop it.

But she wouldn't.

CHAPTER SIX

*P*hoenix checked his phone. Again. No communication from Mack all day. He hoped for at least a text to see if he'd started the work at her house, but she either trusted him completely or didn't care if he'd shown up. He was gambling on the first one.

He locked the front door of her house and pocketed the extra key. The projects on her house were extensive. He could keep busy for a year here, but he would do the basic stuff to add some equity to her home. He was never going to take her money. A real man didn't help the woman he cared about for a paycheck. He could never tell her that. She'd slap him.

The sky was filled with gray clouds. They might see some snow or ice. The damp ocean air made his knee ache. He limped to his truck. He'd like to patch Mack's roof, but he couldn't climb up there with one bad leg. He shouldn't even be climbing up a ladder, but he was never one to do as he was told, which is what had snarled him in the mess in the elementary school.

They were told to call for help before the tanks started beeping. There was no way he would do that and let the guys bust on him for panicking. Like the new kid, Tim. Tim had freaked out; his tank was full, and Phoenix was standing right next to him. That was a year and a half ago. No one ever let Tim hear the end of it.

He slid into the truck and debated on sending Mack a text.

Buying supplies today. Projects begin tomorrow. The text was delivered, but the response bubble didn't pop up. She was probably busy. Or she was ignoring him.

Last night he had wanted to pull her into his arms and kiss the hell out of her, but she had stayed on her side of the couch with her arms crossed over her chest. He had been pretty sure she liked the kiss in the kitchen. He sure had. His heart had pounded against his ribs and had made it hard to breathe.

He hadn't wanted to force her. She would set the pace. But when she took off her sweatshirt and only had that tank on underneath, showing off her sculpted arms, it took all his resolve not to touch her. Because if he had so much as felt a wisp of her skin against his, he would've wanted to make love to her all night.

His phone vibrated against the cup holder. The caller's name popped up on the dashboard screen. He hit the accept button.

"Hey, Hawk. What's up?"

"Where the hell are you?"

"I said tonight." He turned in the direction of his brother's house instead of the hardware store.

"Not tonight. This afternoon. I want that crib built

before Aria gets home so I can surprise her. Can you come now?"

"I need to be done by four." He wanted to get back to Mack's when she got home. He could show her his plans for her upgrades. Simple stuff, but it would add value.

"Bring lunch." Hawk ended the call.

He turned the truck around again.

"CAN YOU HAND ME THAT SCREWDRIVER?" Hawk held out his hand.

Phoenix put his sub down. The crib was almost finished. The walls had been painted a pale green. Stuffed pigs, monkeys, and smiling moons filled a white rope hammock hanging in the corner of the nursery.

"You ready for this?" He slapped the screwdriver into Hawk's hand.

Hawk looked up at him from his spot under the crib. "To be done building furniture? Yeah, I'm ready. That rocking chair took me all damn day. I wanted to throw it out the window by the time I was done. It's made like shit, but don't tell Aria. She loved it. She's been sitting in it every day, reading to the baby."

"I meant being a dad." He sat at the window seat and picked at the lettuce that had fallen onto the wax paper.

A few years ago, he hadn't been sure if Hawk would find his way out of a bottle. Wyatt's death had crushed him, and there had been nothing Phoenix could do to save his kid brother. Aria's leaving Hawk had been the thing to snap him out of it.

"A father? No way. What do I know about being a dad?" Hawk pushed off the ground and dumped the screwdriver into the toolbox. The tools clanked in protest. "It wasn't as if we had the best example."

He thought the same thing about himself. If things actually worked out between him and Mack, the boys were part of the package. They were great, but did he really know how to handle the tough stuff? He could barely handle his own shit.

"You aren't anything like him. Never think that. You're going to be a good dad." Hawk was the one made of the stuff good fathers came from.

"I hope so. I can't back out now." He shrugged. "I wish I could tell Wyatt. He would've had a good laugh of it."

"Yeah, he would've." The hole in his heart where his big brother used to be ached like a fresh wound. "Can I ask you something?"

"Do I have a choice?" Hawk bit into his sub. Shredded lettuce and tomato dropped out of the bun and onto the wax paper below it.

He hesitated. He could trust Hawk. They were all they had left. Well, Hawk was all the family he had left. The guys at the firehouse were like his family too, but only Hawk knew what it was like to suffer the way they had.

"After Wyatt, how did you go back to work?" He turned his gaze out the window. Watching the sun through the bare tree branches was easier than meeting Hawk's stare.

"Are you forgetting about all my mistakes? I didn't go back to work for months."

"I know, but the first time you put on the gear and

hopped on the truck. Were you scared?" He had never asked Hawk about his feelings on his first day back.

"Hell yeah, I was scared. I threw up." Hawk tore off another piece of his sub.

"You did?" He had been there Hawk's first day back but hadn't seen him getting sick.

"I didn't want to fuck up again. I know Wyatt didn't die because of me. That floor would've collapsed anyway, but I still wake up sweating, thinking if I hadn't needed him, he would've been somewhere else in that building. He might still be alive now. Why are you bringing this up?" Hawk gathered their garbage. Phoenix followed Hawk out of the room and to the kitchen.

He should admit that he didn't want to go back to work. Every time he thought about stepping into the complete blackness, a room filled with eight-hundred-degree heat, the only way to breathe was through his mask, he broke out in a sweat. His stomach cramped, and his head hurt. How could his men rely on him if he couldn't trust himself?

"I've been thinking about Wyatt a lot lately." Not a total lie. He thought about his brother all the time.

Hawk stopped with his hand hovering over the stain-less-steel garbage can. "What's going on?"

"What do you mean?"

"Your tank was less than one minute from running out of air when we were at the school. I kept the time because I was ready to run back in and get you when you didn't come out with the students. I figured you were lost and didn't want to say. I had no intention of losing another brother. But at the last second, I found you in the hallway holding that rabbit. I didn't say anything because you seemed okay till you fell down the steps. Are you thinking you can't go in?" Hawk dumped the trash and washed his hands.

"I'm fine." He leaned on the chairback, but kept his gaze away.

"Don't lie to me. If you can't go in, you need to get to a therapist now. I don't give a shit what the other guys say. You're the toughest one in our group. This doesn't change that."

He needed to back-pedal this conversation before he gave away too much. "You're wrong. I'm fine. The only thing bothering me is my knee. Once that's healed up, I'll be back on the job."

"There's no shame in needing help. Isn't that what we tell the guys at our grief retreat?"

This wasn't the same thing. No one had died on that shift at the school. For some guys, when they lost a brother or a father or an uncle in a fire, it froze them. They can't handle the pain or the pressure. They question why they were even fighting anymore. It wasn't like that for him. He could handle it. He just needed some time.

"I have to hit the road. Mack should be back at her house by now." He reached for his jacket.

Hawk eyed him. "Phoenix, man, don't take this on by yourself."

"Little brother, if I need your help, I'll ask. But there isn't a problem with me and my job." He might have a win for the time being, but Hawk wasn't stupid. His brother would catch on if he wasn't careful.

"You're spending a lot of time with Mack lately." Hawk pushed off the counter and followed him to the door.

"She needs some work done around the house. I don't mind helping her." He wouldn't say anything about the custody battle, but Mack must've told Aria by now. He also wasn't going to mention the kiss. He had promised to be discreet. He might not be a lot of things, but he was a man of his word.

"You're taking on work with that knee? And you didn't mention it to me?"

"Working with you is a real pain in my ass. I don't know why I agreed to go into contracting with you. I need my own space. I can handle the work." He fished his keys out of his jacket pocket.

"If you bust up that knee worse, then you can't come back to your real job. We need you. The new guy is a big baby." Hawk opened the front door and headed out to the porch.

The sun set behind the housetops and washed the sky of its color. The breeze picked up off the ocean. The fresh air did him some good. So would seeing Mack.

"I won't let anything happen to my leg. I'll be back to work soon." He hobbled down the steps.

Guilt pressed on his chest like a coiled firehose. He couldn't allow some new guy to mess up the energy of his team, but if he forced himself to go back now, he wasn't sure what the panic attacks would be like. He needed a little more time.

"Oh, by the way, the chief told me to tell you the parade committee wants you to make a speech at the end."

Hawk's words stopped him in his tracks.

"Hell no. Why are they having a parade in January anyway?"

"Beats me. They want your ugly face out in the cold waving to the tax payers. So, I'll tell him you'll do it. Or you can call him yourself. I'm not your secretary though everyone seems to think I am."

"Can you tell him for me?" It wasn't fair to take advantage of Hawk this way, but he didn't want to talk to the chief. Chief might also be able to detect his concerns about returning to work.

"Oh, fuck. Okay. I'm always getting suckered into your stuff. No speech. Just the parade."

"I don't want to be in any parade."

"No one does, but thanks to you, we are. Let's just get it over with. Then we can go back to normal."

Whatever that was.

CHAPTER SEVEN

*M*ack popped David's name into the search engine and checked over her shoulder. Elliott and Ian played in their rooms. She didn't want them to come in and recognize their father's name on the screen.

The search didn't show much. His property tax record and a few name and address records. David didn't believe in social media. He had always made her feel foolish for posting pictures of things she baked or things the boys did. She had basically gone off-line while they were married just to keep some peace. She let out a long breath. She still had trouble wrapping her head around the fact she had allowed him to steal so much of herself.

She knew little about his past. He had to have attended a military academy in order to be an officer, but she didn't know which one. He never wanted any of his diplomas or medals hung up. He had said those papers didn't mean anything. What meant something to him was the hard work he did with his platoons. Saving lives meant something. He was proud of that.

But she did know his parents' names and searched for them. They had died before she and David met, but he'd taken her to their graves once in northern New Jersey. His mother had died of cancer, and his father, so heartbroken by it, died six months later. That was the kind of love Mack imagined. Her parents didn't have it. Her mother had hated her father so much, she left four girls behind and hightailed it out of town never to be heard from again. Blair had found her once, but their mother had been clear. Family wasn't for her.

She checked the time. Phoenix would be here soon. He'd sent a text that he was leaving Hawk's and coming by. Her heart picked up speed at the idea of him back in her house. Fear and desire mixed like melted butter and eggs. She had replayed that kiss a hundred times. All that accomplished was wanting more and created worry someone would find out what they were doing.

The search for David's parents provided a separate obituary for Marcus and Beverly Hubert. The dates matched the ones she had seen. She clicked on Beverly's. She had been survived by her husband and three sons. No names for the children were listed.

"Mommy, come see what I drew." Elliott called from his bedroom.

"Okay, buddy." She really needed to stop having conversations across the house.

"Mommy, now."

She heaved out of the chair and wrapped her ugly, tattered cardigan around her. She had better discard this rag before Phoenix arrived. He wouldn't want to be kissing her looking like a mess.

She stopped outside Ian's door first. The door was ajar. She gave it a light push. "Hey, pal. Whatcha doing?"

Ian jumped. "Nothing."

She went into the room and took a glance around. "What do you have there?"

His little faced crumpled. "Am I in trouble?"

She squatted down to his level. "Of course not. We just don't keep secrets in this house, remember?"

"I wanted to hide a present for Elliott." He handed over his favorite toy train.

"Where were you going to put it?" Her heart squeezed at the idea her little boy wanted to share his prized possession with his twin.

"I want to put it in there." He pointed to the grate covering the heating duct at the bottom of the wall.

"You can't hide things in there. That's where the heat comes from. Let's find another place to put it."

"But that's where Daddy hides presents."

"No, he doesn't."

"He does. I saw it when I was playing on the floor. My train hit the part that looks like this, and it moved. I pushed it to the side by accident. I didn't mean to, but I could see inside. Will Daddy get mad I found his present? I'm sorry." Tears filled his eyes.

She gripped his tiny shoulders. "You didn't do anything wrong. Do you hear me? It was an accident. Does Daddy know you found his spot?"

Hiding something inside a heating duct made no sense. Ian could have seen it wrong, but he rarely confused details even at his age. He was the one who could repeat what someone said exactly as he heard it. If Elliott had told her this same story, she would chalk it up to a child's imagination.

"I didn't tell him. I didn't want him to be mad."

Because David could be scary when he was mad. She had often tip-toed around him just to keep peace.

"Okay, this can be our secret. Don't even tell Elliott. Promise me, buddy. Just you and me on this one."

"I won't tell. I can keep a secret." He sat up straighter and emphasized his point with a nod.

"You sure can." She kissed the top of his head.

David had a safe in his office which he would never give her the combination to when she lived there too. Why would David hide something in the wall now when he was the only adult in the house?

"Do you want to go to Daddy's house this weekend?" This weekend David was going to take the boys. She had to let them go, but she worried he wouldn't bring them back. She couldn't trust him. What if he tried to run with them? All those crime shows twisted her thoughts into something ugly.

"Mommy, where are you?" Elliott ran into Ian's room and grabbed her hand. "Come on. I want to show you something. Hi, Ian."

"Hi, Elliott." Ian plopped onto his bed. His face was scrunched up.

"Elliott, Mommy is talking to Ian. I'll be there in a minute." She needed to know if Ian wanted to be with David. Had something happened the last time that had her serious child worked up?

"No, now. You're always too busy." Elliott stuck out his bottom lip.

The doorbell rang, shattering the heated scene.

"I'll get it." Elliott bounded out of the room on spinning feet.

"Elliott Hubert, don't you dare open that door without me. Ian, we'll finish talking later." She hurried after Elliott.

Elliott had opened the door anyway. The cold air swooped in and around her legs before she turned the corner. She was ready to reprimand him about safety and stranger danger, but Phoenix's smile and the grocery bag in his hand stopped her.

That smile took her breath away. She was naive enough to hope he only smiled at her that way.

"Hey," he said.

"Mom, it's Aunt Aria's brother." Elliott jumped up and down on socked feet and pointed.

"Thank you for letting me know who's here, but Phoenix is Uncle Hawk's brother not Aunt Aria's." She tried to still her jumping bean.

"Better that way," Phoenix said with a wink.

"Hi." She soaked in his flannel shirt hanging over his jeans and those thick legs.

She tugged at her sweater to keep the cold away and stifled a groan. Not only did she have the old, frayed sweater on, but her hair was piled on her head because she needed to get it off her face. She hadn't showered since she'd been home. She probably smelled like the bakery, and she had hoped to run a toothbrush over her teeth before he got here.

"Can I come in?" He held up the bags.

"Oh, I'm sorry. Yes." She had been so preoccupied with her thoughts she hadn't realized she'd left him on the porch. Even Elliott had disappeared somewhere.

"You look great. I haven't eaten. I hope you don't mind burgers."

"You didn't have to do that." She took one of the bags from him and unloaded the contents onto the counter.

He leaned in and kissed her cheek. The smell of clean cotton and a hint of musk knocked her off-balance. She wanted to stick her nose against his neck and inhale until her head spun.

"Please don't do that." She eased away. Her heart yelled for her to shut up and take the kiss.

"Was it wrong?"

"I thought you were coming to tell me what you found today and how much it would cost me." She didn't know how to navigate her feelings. She wanted to be with him, had been thinking about it all day.

Maybe it was what Ian had just told her that had her rattled. Or maybe the idea of David catching her in an intimate relationship shut her stomach down.

"We can talk about the house all night, but that was an innocent kiss hello. Friends do that kind of thing." He pulled groceries from the bag.

"You kiss all your friends?"

"Just the pretty ones." He continued to unload his bag.

"Phoenix, we need to set up some boundaries. When the boys are home and awake, no touching." She checked for the sound of fast-moving feet, but everything seemed quiet for the moment.

"Your ex-husband doesn't have the right to take your

happiness away." He faced her head-on and held her gaze. The intense glare made her feet shift. She did not need to be afraid. What did it say if she were?

"He can take my boys, though. I don't even want to hint that I'm in any kind of relationship right now." It was too soon to define what was happening between them. Until now they were friends, but the kiss changed things. If he hadn't kissed her, she would have been fine keeping her fantasies to herself until some other woman came along and snagged him.

"Would it be so bad to have a committed, healthy relationship with a man who cares about you?" He leaned on the counter with both hands.

"David will turn something sweet and innocent around. He'll say I'm not paying attention to the boys. He'll say I'm selfish. And maybe I am. My first priority has to be my children. There is no place in my life for a romance. Putting my needs ahead of my children's would make me a terrible mother. When they're older and don't need me as much, that's when I can think about me." She folded the brown grocery bags into neat rectangles.

"I realize I'm not an expert in this subject, but plenty of people have children and lives of their own. You can do both. I can help you." He placed a warm hand over her cold one.

"You don't have to take on parenting." She relished the small touch between them.

"You're going to push me away before we've given this a chance. I promised to keep this a secret even though I don't like that idea. We have nothing to be ashamed of." He waved his arm in the air.

"Please lower your voice." She checked again to make sure the coast was clear.

He slammed the loaf of bread down. She jumped.

"I'm sorry. I didn't mean to scare you." He ran a hand over his face. "Please don't do this." His words were a whisper.

Pain etched lines around his mouth. It could be his knee, but he couldn't have been expecting her to say the things she had been saying. She had sent him mixed messages with that kiss. She had been sending herself mixed messages too.

"Why is being with me so important? You could have any woman you wanted."

"Thanks for the vote of confidence, but that isn't true. I don't want any other woman. I like how I feel when I'm with you. When I'm not with you, I just want to get back to you so I can feel that way again. Is that so bad?"

Far from it. She couldn't have asked for a better answer because that was how she felt too. Her feelings for him had snuck up on her when she wasn't expecting them. She owed him a piece of honesty.

"I'm afraid." The truth hurt like a burn from a cookie sheet. She was terrified of what David would do if he could prove she was an unfit mother, and she was afraid to watch Phoenix walk away.

"Have a little faith, Mack. I'd never do anything to hurt you or your children. I get it that we have to keep things quiet, and even take it slow, which believe me won't be easy. Every time I see you, I want to kiss the hell out of you. Then undress you until you're lying beneath me. But I'll do whatever you ask. Just don't ask me to go."

"You're a great guy." The declaration fell flat. It wasn't what she meant to say. She wanted to tell him how easy he was to talk to or how sweet he was with her boys or how she admired his kindness.

"But?" The lines around his mouth deepened.

If this had been even a month ago, she would have gone for it, full force. But with the custody battle hanging over her head, she had too much to lose.

"I can't lose my children. It would be the end of me."

"I won't let that happen."

"You can't stop it." His presence and the way he made her feel jeopardized her heart, her soul, and her case.

"Wouldn't it be better to go through this with someone you can trust?"

She had plenty of reasons to trust him, but the words died on her lips. Every time she had trusted someone in the past, she had paid. Losing her children was too big a ticket. She had to wait, and if he was still available when this was all over, she'd beg him to give her another chance.

"Your silence says it all. Enjoy the food."

It was just like Phoenix to give her what she wanted even if he was mad about it.

Why then, did it hurt so much to breathe?

CHAPTER EIGHT

*M*ack locked the bakery door. The last customer had finally left. She needed to bake a cake for a bridal shower before she could go home. The boys were set up at the table with new coloring books she had purchased earlier. She needed them to sit quietly for an hour. She'd decorate the cake tomorrow.

She hadn't been focused all day which was why she still needed to bake that cake. The only thing she could think about was Phoenix walking out of the house. The hurt in his eyes when he looked at her made her heart stick in her throat. She hadn't wanted him to go, but she didn't see any other choice.

Elliott and Ian giggled while they shared crayons. They were her existence. She would die for them. She couldn't let anything get in the way of her relationship with her boys. That included the man who had piqued her interest like no other.

She turned on the Michael Grimm album and let his

soulful voice drift around her. "Boys, I'll be right in the kitchen."

The pounding on the door made her head swing around before she could take a step.

"Daddy." Ian leapt from the chair and ran to the door.

Elliott hurried after his brother and tugged at the handle.

Her stomach hollowed out. She shooed the boys away from the door and unlocked it. "David, what are you doing here?" She had hoped to avoid any additional meetings with him.

He pushed his way in. The boys clung to his legs. He pried their little arms away. "What are you trying to pull, Mack?" The snarl on David's lip said this situation would erupt. The boys didn't need to be a part of it.

"Boys, Daddy and I need to talk. Go in the back."

"Stay where you are." He pointed a finger at each boy.

"Don't talk to them like that." She stepped between David and the boys.

He leaned into her personal space with eyes the size of cake pans. "I will talk to them anyway I want. They are my children. Today is my day. I went to the school, and they said you took them."

"Today isn't your day. It's Friday." If she didn't know better, she'd swear he was joking. Except something closer to rage masked his face instead of humor.

She stole a glance out the windows. Streaks of gray painted Main Street as the sun set on another day. No one was out there walking around. No one would walk in and interrupt them.

"Daddy, are you and Mommy having a fight?" Elliott tugged on David's coat.

"No, sweetie," she said.

"Yes, we are. Fighting is what happens when mommies and daddies don't like each other anymore." David bore his gaze into hers even though he spoke to Elliott.

His message was clear. She needed to get him out of there without causing too much trouble for herself. She tried to still her racing heart first.

Elliott's face crumpled. "I fought with Ian today. Does he still love me?"

"David, what are you trying to do? The boys don't need to be a part of this," she hissed.

"You're right. I'll put them in the car."

"No. They stay here. It's too cold to wait in the car." She could continue the argument that it wasn't his day, but the boys needed to be out of earshot.

She ushered them to the table and gave them each a crayon. She kissed their heads and moved to the far corner of the bakery where the windows went from ceiling to floor.

"We agreed I would start taking them on Friday nights after school," David said.

"We never agreed to that." She would never have given in to that request without a court order.

"This is the problem. You can't keep a schedule. I'm surprised you get the boys to school at all. In our last phone conversation, I specifically stated I wanted the boys on Fridays too and you said you were fine with it. In fact, you wanted the time to yourself."

She was already afraid David would take the boys at

his regularly scheduled time and never give them back. Any extra time with him only worried her. She would gladly give up her free time to keep the boys away from their father.

"David, I think you're mistaken." She tried to keep her voice calm. If she appeared scared or angry, he would try and use it against her. He would twist what she said until she didn't recognize her own words.

"Why would I make that mistake?"

"I'm sure it's just a misunderstanding."

"Mackenzie, I don't make mistakes like that. That's what you do. You run late. You forget things. You're irresponsible. That's why the boys will be living with me soon. Where they should be." He shoved his finger in her face.

"I know what day you have the boys." She tilted her chin and shoved his hand away, but her bowels turned to ice water.

"You can't keep the boys from me." His face blossomed red. He shook his head and took a step back. "What will the judge say when I tell him you went back on our agreement? He isn't going to be happy that you won't hold up your end of the bargain." His voice shifted from angry to condescending.

"This isn't your day." Her voice shook. He was making it all up, yet she started to doubt herself. She wanted to check her phone's calendar, but wouldn't pull it out in front of him.

"You know what? I'll come back for the boys tomorrow." He threw his hands in the air. "I'll just tell my lawyer you wouldn't give me the boys on our regularly scheduled time, and when I tried to ask nicely, you only managed to get nuts. Like you always do."

"I'm not nuts." Her throat tightened, and her fists clenched.

"Really? What's with the yelling? You don't see me losing my temper. It's always you who starts it. I came here worried about where the boys were, or that maybe you had done something with them."

"What would I have done with my own children?"

"I don't know with you. I don't trust you to take care of them."

"How can you say any of this? No matter what's happened between us, I've never doubted you loved them." She fought the urge to scream because reasoning with him wasn't going to get her anywhere.

"I believe you love them. You just aren't fit to take care of them."

"You're crazy. I don't understand where any of this is coming from. Get out of my bakery."

"Never say those words to me." He gripped her arm.

"Let go of me." She tugged her arm, but he held harder.

"I'll call my lawyer when I leave here and tell him you are holding the kids against their will." His fingers bit into her skin.

"Go ahead. Let go of me, I said." She willed her voice to stay calm.

"Boys, do you want to come sleep at Daddy's tonight?" He pulled her arm down so the boys couldn't see he had a grip on her.

He had done that to her so many times before. He hurt her just enough no one would notice. He was doing it again with the custody battle. She wanted to be sick over her stupidity where this man had been concerned.

"Yes." They shouted together.

"Is everything okay here?"

Her head spun at the sound of the deep male voice in her store. She hadn't noticed the door open or the cold air swirling in. Phoenix stood there with his hands on his hips. The cold stare in his eyes would freeze the ocean.

David released her and moved away. She resisted the urge to rub her arm. Heat burned her cheeks, but she forced her head to stay high and meet Phoenix's gaze. The cold stare melted when he looked at her.

"Everything's fine." She hoped she sounded confident. Her heart racing made her want to vomit and destroy any chance of looking strong and secure.

"My wife and I are having a personal discussion. Come back tomorrow for your bakery items."

"She's your ex-wife, pal. From the street, things didn't look fine. Mack, do you need anything?"

She needed David to go. Then she needed Phoenix to follow so she could have a proper breakdown.

"She doesn't need anything from you," David said.

"I wasn't asking you. Mack?" Phoenix moved closer and held her gaze. She wanted to run to him, but stayed put.

"No, thank you. Everything is fine here. Did you want some pastries? I still have some left." She needed to act as if this was any other customer. David couldn't know she had feelings for Phoenix other than friendship. The boys stared on with wide eyes.

"I'll wait." Phoenix went over to the boys and gave them high fives.

"I'll be leaving with my children, and if you're good, I'll bring them back Sunday night as we discussed. That means don't call this weekend to talk to the boys. I want some alone time with them. If you interrupt that, I'll keep them until Monday or longer. I can do it. No one will deny me my time."

"We never agreed to Friday nights." She kept her voice low.

"Would you like to start a scene in front of your friend? I'm happy to make one."

"You're a shit."

How was she going to go two full days without talking to the boys? If she said no now, the boys would be hurt and mad at her. And if she had screwed up the days, because what if she had, then David would have something to hold against her. She didn't want to make a scene in front of Phoenix either. He would come to her defense, which might prove bad for David.

David stared at her with a smug look on his face. She wanted to slap it off.

"Boys…." She cleared her throat and started again. "Boys, Daddy is taking you home with him tonight for the whole weekend." She clapped her hands as if this was a big surprise she had been in all along.

Her sentence was met with squeaky cheers. The boys tumbled out of their chairs, gave her quick hugs, and grabbed David's hands.

"Remember what I said. We'll see you Sunday night,

but that's up to you. Well, it's up to you for the next three weeks."

"What do you mean?"

"I guess you didn't check your email again. Our court date has been set for three weeks from today. Good night." He ushered the boys out to the street.

Elliott gave her a final wave from the sidewalk before the big car swallowed them up and drove away. She slumped against the counter. Her legs gave up their job, and she slid to the floor, having been verbally beaten by her ex-husband. Again.

"Hey." Phoenix put out a hand, but she refused it. He made his way next to her, favoring his bad leg.

"You don't have to sit here with me. In fact, you should go." Tears threatened to come, and she wanted to have herself a good cry, but she bit them back because she could not fall apart in front of Phoenix.

"I'm not leaving you and will stay for however long you need me to." He laced his fingers through hers.

"I have to find something to use against him. He's going to take my children from me." His strong hands holding hers gave her the strength to let the air out of her lungs.

"He won't win." His thumb caressed the top of her hand.

"Really? How am I going to stop that? The war veteran who has his act together versus the single mother who lives in a run-down bungalow, can't remember what day of the week it is, and won't honor the original custody agreement?"

"It's not enough to stick, Mack. What you're saying about yourself isn't true."

"He came in here accusing me of messing up our days. I don't remember talking about a new arrangement, but maybe I did. Maybe just to make him go away I told him he could have them, and I've forgotten. I'm always forgetting things. I forget to pick them up at school."

She was losing her mind. She didn't know what was right and wrong anymore. This could be all her fault. It was her fault. She had married David in the first place.

"I think what's happening here is you see yourself the way David wants you to. This is how I see you. You're a good mother. You love those kids. You take care of them. You're there for them. A mess-up once in a while means you're human."

"David is using it against me. I don't have anything to accuse him of. On paper, he's perfect."

"Can I ask you something?"

"That sounds like I might not like it." She stole a glance at him.

"Did I walk in on what I thought I saw?" He kept his head straight. His strong jaw clenched, but he never let go of her hand.

Heat burned her cheeks again. She couldn't look at him. "What did you think you saw?"

"He had his hands on you in a way that wasn't cool."

"Phoenix, I didn't need you to step in and save me." She could handle David. No one had to be the knight on the white horse. Fairy tales weren't real.

"I know you can handle yourself, but it made me mad

when I saw his hands on you. He's a bully, Mack. I hate bullies."

Her tongue tied around the embarrassment. She was smart. She should've seen David coming a mile away, but she hadn't. She had fallen for him like a love sick girl. She couldn't stand herself sometimes.

He turned to her. "Can you look at me?"

She forced her gaze to his. His dark eyes were filled with kindness. He smiled, and she was lost in his light. "This isn't about you. He's a dick who needs his ass kicked."

The tears spilled down her face. He wiped them away with a soft touch. She leaned her head against his shoulder and drank in his strength. "I don't know what to do."

"Has he ever hurt the boys?"

"No." But what if that changed? What if this was the weekend that he hit one of them? Who would protect them if David had them full time? She couldn't let that happen. She couldn't survive without her boys.

"How bad has he hurt you?"

"Bad enough." The details didn't matter. She never wanted the kindness in Phoenix's eyes replaced with pity.

"Who knows?" He shifted on the floor and rubbed his leg above the bandage.

"No one. I never told a soul." Which had been a mistake. "Let's get off this floor. It can't be good for you, and my butt is cold."

"Hey," he held her shoulders. "We'll find something else to get him on."

She stood and gave him a hand. "This isn't your fight."

Her body ached. A hot bath and a glass of wine would help.

"You don't have to do it alone."

"Do you know what I could really use right now?" Besides a hot bath and a hot firefighter in her bed.

"Whatever you need." He cocked his brow.

She laughed in spite of her situation. He was the one person who could make her forget her troubles for a little while. When she was with him, he gave her the strength to believe she was safe.

"I have to bake a cake, or I'm going to lose an important customer. I can't let that happen."

"You want me to assist?"

"Well, I was thinking maybe grab us some dinner and a bottle of wine. I'll be done in an hour."

"You don't trust my baking skills?" He faked a pout.

"How many cakes have you baked?"

"None. But I follow directions pretty good."

"Maybe another time for the cake. It will go faster if I do it. But afterward, you could take me home." She didn't want to be alone tonight. The wine would give her courage.

"I'll be back in an hour."

And she'd be ready.

CHAPTER NINE

*P*hoenix pulled up to the bakery with two bottles of wine and a pizza. Mack had basically propositioned him, but he wouldn't take advantage of her vulnerability. He wished he could throw his principles under the truck, but she meant too much to him. He wanted to make love to her, but when the time was right. Not when David had made her doubt herself.

She came out of the bakery and locked the door behind her. She gave him a small wave, and his heart flipped on its head. He should've asked her out sooner. He'd been a coward. If he hadn't waited, they would already be a couple fighting her ex together.

"Hey." She slid into the passenger seat. "Ooh. Pizza. I'm starved."

"How did the cake go?"

"I don't know. I hope it doesn't taste like cardboard. My mind wasn't on my work. Thank you for taking care of dinner and me. I really try not to fall apart in front of anyone."

She had no idea how much he wanted to take care of her. He never wanted to interfere with her independence. That stubborn streak was the exact thing that kept him up at night with desire for her. But he wanted to make her happy because when she smiled at him, everything else didn't matter. If she didn't have so much going on in her life, he might consider telling her about his concerns with returning to work. She was all the therapy he needed.

"You're safe with me. If you fall apart, I'll catch the pieces. Sorry. That was kind of cheesy." He backed out of the parking spot.

"Not at all." She took his hand in her cold one. He squeezed, and she squeezed back.

He was in trouble. If he continued to touch her, he wouldn't want to stop.

They drove through town in silence. She must be able to hear the pounding of his heart inside the quiet truck. He stole a glance at her. She rested her head against the seat and closed her eyes. Even like that, the stress of what she was going through left marks on her beautiful face.

Her house came into view under the streetlamp. The windows were dark. The house absent of its light and warmth seemed sad. Like its owner. He pulled into the driveway and turned off the truck. It wasn't too late to give her the pizza and the wine and leave her alone. She'd be better off without him distracting her tonight.

"I'll grab the food." He opened the door and slid out. So much for leaving her alone.

She unlocked the front door and began turning on lights. The house's sadness retreated into the corners of the rooms. Mack needed some of what made her unhappy shoved away too. He deposited the food on the counter in the kitchen.

She came into the room pulling her scarf from her neck. "I just turned up the heat. It's cold in here."

Her windows were old and needed to be replaced. That would add more value to her house. It was one of the projects he wanted to tackle. "I can add some insulation to the attic."

"Not if that's extra." She grabbed plates.

"It's no big deal. I have extra from another project. Hawk won't mind if I use some of it." That was a complete lie, but he would never tell her that. Insulation wouldn't cost that much.

Growing up, money had always been tough. His mother never held much of a job before she left them. His father had to raise three boys on a firefighter's salary. That didn't go very far in an expensive state like New Jersey, and there was his problem with buying booze over food.

Once Phoenix started working, he banked every penny. Being frugal was the reason he'd bought that old truck instead of a new one. He could afford to spot Mack a few projects.

"Are you sure your knee can take it? You've been limping a lot."

"I'm fine. But thanks for asking. Let's eat." He plopped a slice on the plate. The cheese slid off.

Mack grabbed it between her fingers before it hit the counter and held it up to him. He tried not to groan with pleasure. He took the cheese between his teeth and tugged her closer. She tilted her head back and laughed. Music to his ears. When she laughed for him, he was the luckiest bastard in the world.

He grabbed her around the waist to pull her against him because even that wasn't close enough. His mouth closed around her fingers, and he sucked. She gasped with wide eyes and a bright smile. He kissed the tips of her fingers. "Did you like that?"

Her cheeks turned a bright cherry red like the start of a fire heating up. She nodded. This time he did groan and took her mouth with his.

He pushed her mouth open with his tongue. He couldn't wait. The need to taste her was too great. She pressed against him as their tongues raced after each other. His head spun as if all the oxygen had been sucked from the room. He had Mack in his arms, and she wanted to be there.

Her hands ran up and down his back. He burned for her to touch him all over, but he had to slow down some, or he'd embarrass himself. She settled her fingers into the back pocket of his jeans. A smile tugged at his lips.

He eased back from the kiss to see her face. Her eyes fluttered opened.

"Is everything okay?" Her words were breathless.

"Better than okay. I like your hands in my pockets. I just want to make sure you're good with this. With us. We don't have to do anything except eat pizza, if that's what you want."

"I do want to eat, but later." She smiled up at him.

"I don't want you to regret this in the morning. You had a bad night. I'm not trying to take advantage of the situation—"

"Phoenix, shut up and make love to me."

SHE WOULD NOT REGRET THIS. She had been waiting for this for months. Every time she turned a corner and he was there, she wondered what it would be like to be his woman. She knew what being his friend felt like, but that had stopped being enough. Now she was ready to take a chance.

Maybe it was because David had shown up and made her feel as if she was less than. He had a unique way of doing that. She wanted to feel desired, special. Even if it was just one night. Who was she kidding? One night with Phoenix would never be enough.

She hoped he would stick to her original request of keeping things quiet, though. They could talk about that later. Now was for them.

She took his hand and led him to the back of the house where her bedroom was. She had a couple of candles on her dresser. She found the lighter and gave them a little light to work with. But only a little. She wanted to see him naked, but she wanted the shadows to hide behind for a while.

He came to her and put his hands on her waist. "I can't get enough of you."

She snaked her arms around his neck and kissed him. His tongue made her mind empty of all the problems she had. Her body responded to his touch, and she longed for more of that.

He tugged her shirt over her head and then his own.

She took in his beauty. Her fingers traced the muscles on his abs before stopping at the top of his jeans. He cupped her breast. She tilted her head back and let out a long breath.

"You're beautiful." He left a trail of kisses from her neck to the top of the lace on her bra. She ran her fingers through his short hair to hold him closer.

He cupped her bottom with the other hand and held her to him. His erection pressed into her belly. She was doing that to him. The knowledge that she could make the confident Phoenix Egan want her, when he could have any woman he wanted, only made the heat between her legs turn up to four hundred degrees. Her oven was cooking.

"Can you take off your pants?" she said.

He eased back and took off the knee brace, then he stepped out of his jeans.

She sucked in a breath. "Is it impolite to say wow?"

His lip curled up in a cocky grin. "I'll take wow."

"Is your knee going to be okay?"

"I'm fine." His erection pressed against his black underwear. She wondered if Aria was this lucky and then shook the thought away.

Her fingers ran over the solid muscle of his thighs. "I've wanted to do that for a while now."

He sucked in a breath. She reached for him through his briefs, but he took her hands in his.

"Can you take off yours too? I've been wanting to run my hands over your legs too."

She slid out of her pants and kicked them to the side.

"My turn to say wow." He pulled her to him again.

They kissed until she wasn't sure her legs would continue to hold her up. His hands ran over her belly and snaked around to her bottom. His grip was strong from the hard work he did. Her insides melted like butter.

She removed her bra and panties wanting to feel his skin against all of hers. He took her cue and stepped out of his briefs, favoring his left leg. She led him to the bed, and he lay beside her. He filled the space as if he belonged there much the way he had belonged in her kitchen helping her to make dinner.

His mouth and hands were all over her, and it wasn't enough. She craved him. He found her breast with his tongue and left hot, wet circles on her nipple. His hand traveled in the direction of the heat in her body. She quivered, waiting for him to go lower.

"Phoenix?" Her mind snarled around her desire. She should keep her mouth shut, but she had been afraid before. She didn't want to be scared anymore.

"Hmm?" He glanced up at her through his long eye lashes. A smile decorated his handsome features.

"Would you tell me if something isn't right? If you don't like something, I mean." David had complained about her love making all the time. She often just wished it would end when he climbed on top of her.

His hand paused on her thigh. "Are you talking about right now?"

"Yeah. I guess." The darkness provided an appreciated cover.

He moved so they could face each other. "Mack, you're blowing my mind right now. I'm trying to take my time and act like a gentleman instead of an ape, but you're so damn sexy I'm struggling by the minute. You don't ever have to worry."

She tried to show him with her kiss how much she wanted him in that moment. He groaned inside the kiss. Her sweet spot heated up more. His hand resumed its decent.

Her hips went up to meet him halfway. His finger slipped inside her and every nerve ending sizzled like a hot skillet. She pressed his hand against her core. Sparks lit up behind her eyelids.

"Shit, Mack, you're so wet. I love it." He ran his mouth and tongue over her neck and shoulder. Her hips matched the rhythm he set.

Her hand circled the width of him and stroked. She savored the feel of his erection and the way he said her name over and over. She wanted him to burn with desire too.

An ache twisted inside her with each kiss and caress that wouldn't be eased until he filled her up. Nothing would satisfy her until he was inside her.

He teased her to the edge of ecstasy, but pulled back before she could fall over.

"Don't stop," she said between short breaths.

"I want to see your face when you come." He moved her hand away from him and laced his fingers through hers.

"You do?" She had always kept her eyes closed when she and David had sex.

"Are you kidding? You bet I do. This whole thing won't matter at all if I can't make you feel like you're soaring. I don't want you to miss the smile on my face when it happens."

She put a hand on his cheek. The stubble on his jaw tickled her skin. "How are you for real?"

He kissed her palm. "Keep your eyes on me."

He slid between her legs and gripped her thigh.

"Are you sure your knee is okay? I can get on top."

"I've got this. If you're comfortable with things this way, this is exactly how I want to stay."

She wrapped her legs around him, more ready than she had ever been for this moment. He entered her, and she called out his name. She wanted to close her eyes and focus on the building sensation where they were joined, but she met his gaze instead. Like he asked. Like she wanted to.

"That's it. Stay with me." He whispered and picked up the pace of his hips.

She matched his movements. The whole time not looking away. The tightening in her core twisted more until she couldn't take it. Her breath came in short spurts. Sweat slicked her skin and his. She ran her tongue over his salty shoulder.

For a second, she worried she might not reach the end. Everything had happened so fast. Her body had been steps ahead of her mind.

"Trust me, Mack." He slipped his hand down between them, and with one touch he brought her to the height of her pleasure.

Holding his gaze, the climax crashed into her and took her breath away. Her body quivered and shook with each wave. She called out his name as tears stung her eyes. Tears made from relief. She floated back down from the incredible ride, leaving kisses on his chin.

He pushed up on his arms and thrust into her. He growled but never stopped watching her until he met her on the other side.

He rested his forehead on hers. "Did you like it?"

"More wow," she said.

He rolled to his side and pulled her against him. She rested her head against his chest. In his arms was where she could find comfort. She had never known peace like this. For a short time, all her problems had washed away.

"I only want to make you happy." He kissed the top of her head.

"That was a good start. Is your knee still okay?" She snuggled closer and inhaled his musky scent.

"You don't have to worry about my leg, but thank you for caring about me. Mack, I mean it. If you ever decide you don't want me around, just say it."

She pushed up on an elbow to get a good look at him. "You've been my friend for as long as I can remember. I will always want you around." The pieces of her life wouldn't fit together the right way if Phoenix wasn't a part of it. How could he even say that?

"Making love changes things. I don't think I can go back to just friends. It might kill me."

She was falling fast for him. If she ever lost him, it would be the end of her too. "But you're still okay with keeping us a secret?" *Please be okay with it.*

"For now."

"Only until the custody case is over. Please, Phoenix, promise me you won't say anything. Not even to Hawk."

"I promise. But I don't like it. I want everyone to know you're with me."

"I don't like it either, but it's temporary." He was everything she ever wanted in a man. And the best part was he had no secrets.

CHAPTER TEN

*P*hoenix whistled around Mack's kitchen. The sun climbed over the horizon and drenched the windows in orange. It made streaks across the wood floors. Right after he stopped by the firehouse this morning, he would get to work on her house. He'd start with that insulation and some caulking in the two bathrooms. The back steps needed reinforcing. He could slap a fresh coat of paint on the walls and swap out her old laminate countertop with something more updated. That should at least get her the loan. Or he'd have Hawk lend her money that was really his. He'd do anything for her. He was hooked. Which was why he was willing to keep their thing a secret. For now.

He rummaged through the cabinets for the coffee. Mack was still asleep. She needed the rest. He smiled, remembering how they spent the late hours of the night. His jeans grew tight as images of her floated through his mind. Sex was better with Mack because she was his friend first. He didn't think that was even possible. Boy, was he wrong.

He should come clean about the panic attacks. He couldn't really start a relationship without telling her about his issues. What if something happened to her bakery, and he couldn't put out the fire?

She worried about him too much. She hadn't stopped asking about his knee all night. No telling what she'd try to do if she thought he couldn't fight fires. He had his problems under control. This morning would prove that. She made him better. Calmer.

He opened the cabinet near the stove. Rows of cookbooks lined the shelves. Most of them had shiny spines with titles that implied they were for baking. One book was worn and old. Its green-and-white fabric spine was ripped at the corners. He pulled that one out and flipped it open. The book was filled with yellowed notebook pages and recipes that were written in a messy script. Many of them jotted down in pencil. Some had notes on the side addressed to Mack.

"Those are Pop's recipes. Would you like me to bake you something?" Mack leaned against the doorjamb. Her hair was messed up. A smile crept along her face. She had put on his flannel shirt. It came to her knees and looked fantastic on her. He couldn't wait to take it off.

"Hey. I'm sorry. I was looking for the coffee. I didn't mean to sneak around." He held up the book before putting it back.

"I don't mind sharing my grandfather's recipes with you." She crossed the room and pulled the book back out. She ran her fingers over the pages. "It's all I have left of him. Every time I bake, I feel like he's right beside me, telling me what to do. Most of the stuff I bake at the store is from this book. I wouldn't be half the baker I am if it wasn't for Pop."

"He would be proud of you. You're continuing his legacy." Mack's parents hadn't been much better than his. Her grandfather had been the one special person in her life. Pop had been a great guy. Everyone loved Pop.

She shrugged. "I don't know what Pop would think of my mess with David. Whatever. I just want the boys to have these someday." She put the book back and grabbed the coffee from the fridge. "Are you hungry?"

"I was hoping to make you breakfast." And maybe take her back to bed.

She started the coffee maker. "I don't eat in the morning. I'm too busy trying to get the boys off to school. I usually grab something at the bakery."

"Can you make an exception today?" He didn't want to go back to reality just yet. The firehouse could wait a little longer.

"I have to get to work and finish that cake. Maggie opened for me again today, but I should be there. You don't have to leave if you want a shower or something. But I'm going to head out in about twenty minutes."

The only shower he wanted at the moment was one with her in it. "I'm going to start working on the house this afternoon. Will it be okay if I'm here when you get back?"

"I'd like that." She crossed the room to him. "I like you standing in my kitchen in just those jeans and no shirt." She ran her fingers over his stomach.

His heart picked up speed. He wrapped her in his arms and placed a kiss on her lips. Wanting more, he took the kiss deeper. His fingers tangled in her hair. She moaned, and all his blood ran south.

"Can you be a little late to work?" he asked between kisses.

"You have some appetite." Her hands went up his back. She dragged her fingers over his skin.

Her touch drove him mad. He hiked her onto the counter. She wrapped her legs around his waist and grinded her panties against his erection. He gripped her bottom to hold her close and ran his tongue over her neck and shoulder. "You taste so good."

"Now, Phoenix." She held his face between her hands.

"Who's the one with the appetite?" He kissed her palm.

Her fingers ran back over his chest. His skin was on fire everywhere her touch had been. She fumbled with the button of his jeans in her haste which only made him harder. He gave her a little help, but she didn't wait to push the denim out of the way and grip him.

His body shivered from the heat of her touch. He took her then, unable to wait a second longer.

Their movements were hurried and messy. His knee complained, but he didn't care. She held onto his shoulders and threw her head back. They had barely started before her muscles clenched around him. Between her climax and his name on her lips, he couldn't hold out any longer. The release slammed into him fast and hard. He held her tight not to collapse on the floor.

She looked up at him through hooded eyes. "I don't know what came over me. I had to have you."

"Any time." He kissed her nose and helped her back to the ground. He would do whatever she wanted whenever she asked.

She took her coffee mug and strutted away. He watched until she was out of sight.

He ran a hand over his face.

She was priceless. And he was completely hooked.

PHOENIX STARED up at the firehouse. The building was built in the late seventeen hundreds. Two garages had been added over the years. The building had been renovated, but the original look remained. The red brick façade was faded from the sun and the years of salt air running over it. But the place was sound and strong. Like the men inside. Like he was once. He opened the door and hoped he was over whatever had gripped him by the balls.

The two trucks sat quiet and ready to go. Voices traveled from the kitchen area. Merle, the chief, Tim, and Hawk were on duty. They'd be having lunch about now. The morning training would be over. This would give him a few minutes to see how well he handled being inside the house.

His boots echoed on the clean floor. His heart kept its normal rhythm. His breathing stayed the same. He ran a hand over the ladder truck's wheel as he walked around the truck and the tanker. He took a deep breath. Nothing. He was fine. One night with Mack had cured him.

"Who the hell is in my house?" Chief Wylie stuck his

bald head out. "Well, I'll be damned. Egan, what the hell are you doing? Hawk, your brother is here."

Chief waddled out to give him a solid handshake and a slap on the back. Chief was about a foot shorter than he was, but he had seen everything in his years on the job. Chief had been the one to tell him about Wyatt and caught him when his knees buckled and he fell to the ground because his big brother was dead. Chief was tougher than a battering ram.

"Hey, Chief."

"What're you doing here?" Hawk wiped his mouth with a napkin. "You come for lunch? 'Cause there ain't enough for you. You'll have to go get your own."

"I'm good."

Hawk went back into the kitchen. At work, they were firefighters first and brothers second. Unless they needed each other. Then Hawk would give his life for him, never mind his lunch. He would do the same. He had Hawk's back no matter what. Hawk was a big reason why he hesitated about coming back to work. The last thing he would ever do was put his baby brother in danger because his sad ass needed saving. Hawk would never get hurt over him. Not while he was breathing.

"Egan, are you resting your leg? I need you back on the shift." The chief dragged him out of his thoughts.

"I'm taking care of it. It should be healed up enough soon. I thought I'd drop by and see what's going on."

"It's been quiet. January is like that."

"How's the new guy?"

Chief swiped at the air. "Don't get me started. Kid always needs time off. His girlfriend calls him all the time. Every time I explain something to him, he forgets what I said five minutes later. I need you back. When you return, I'm going to recommend he think about another line of work. Something with not so much pressure. I'm always worried he's going to hurt someone or himself."

"Can't Hawk show him around?" He glanced at his brother.

"I'm trying," Hawk said between bites.

It was his fault this kid was even here. He couldn't let someone on his team get hurt because of him. He had to return to work sooner than he hoped. "How soon can I come back?"

"Get a doctor's note. You can come back tomorrow." Chief's face lit up like the lights on the truck.

Tomorrow. He could do tomorrow. The doctor might fit him in today. He'd have to get to Mack's later than he planned. He couldn't let her down either.

The call alert blared and shook him to the core. The computer screens came to life. "House Fifty, four-alarm house fire at..." Two stories. People might be trapped. The smoke would be black and thick.

The men scrambled into their gear. They ran around him like the debris in a tornado. He couldn't move. His heart slammed against his chest, preventing his lungs from taking in air. Sweat broke out over his skin.

"Egan, do you want to ride with us?" Chief's voice came at him down a dark tunnel.

He shook his head to clear the black, fuzziness around his vision. Hawk slapped him on the shoulder.

"Phoenix. Did you hear me?" Hawk stood in front of

him with a set jaw and held his gaze. Hawk didn't release the grip on his shoulder.

His brother knew. He needed to respond before Hawk said something else.

"I think I'll pass on this one. I don't want to mess up my knee. I'll wait till you're gone and lock up." He forced his legs to keep him standing, but his thighs trembled. His stomach wanted to reject the cups of coffee turning to sludge.

Hawk gave him a quick nod and jumped on the truck. They pulled out with sirens roaring. He waited until the sounds faded away and dropped into a chair.

No other way around it—he was fucked.

CHAPTER ELEVEN

*M*ack let herself into the cold, empty house. The sun was ready to punch its time clock for the day. Long shadows draped over her furniture. She turned on lights as she dropped her bag, kicked off her boots, and tossed her phone on the kitchen table.

The house creaked and groaned as the wind shoved its way off the ocean and through the drafts in her home. She turned up the heat and longed for a fire. She was too tired to be bothered. Her back ached from standing for hours. She had decorated the bridal shower cake and helped Carlos with the rest of the baking for the store. Hiring him had been the best decision she had ever made. Carlos could make breads and cookies like no one's business. People came from surrounding towns for Carlos's breads. He showed up every day, smiled, never complained, and worked like a dog.

Dinner would be peanut butter out of the jar. She didn't have the strength for more, and she still had work to do. She needed to find something to use against David.

Phoenix hadn't called or texted all day. She had checked a million times. Every customer who pushed through the bakery door had her craning her neck for his smile. A glance at the kitchen counter made her blush. She'd never done it on the counter before. He seemed into it as much as she was. He couldn't have had a change of heart that quickly, could he have? That was nonsense talking. She needed to remember he wasn't David. Phoenix must've been busy all day.

The house looked the way she'd left it this morning. He had mentioned he would start the work today. There wasn't a sign anyone had been here. She needed him to get going so she could apply for the loan. Her credit card was maxed out, and Virginia would want more money soon.

David hadn't called either. She missed the boys. Her fingers hovered over the phone. Would David really hold them hostage another night if she called? She knew the answer and didn't like it. She hit the call button anyway.

The phone rang and rang. Of course, he would see it was her and send her to voicemail. She was about to hang up when the call connected.

"Mackenzie, I told you not to call. This is my weekend with the boys. If they had seen your name on the phone, they would've wanted to speak with you." His voice cut through her.

"Why is talking to me such a problem for you? If you're so convinced you're the better parent, I shouldn't be a threat." A hello would've been nice. She expected too much.

"I don't want them confused."

"Oh, get off it. They understand we live in different homes. They aren't confused." It had been recently that Ian wanted David and not her. Ian had expected his father that day after school. Was juggling them between two houses at such a young age too much for them? Or was David making her think she was crazy again?

"Why is following my instructions too much for you?"

"Stop talking to me like I'm a child." She smacked the table. Her heart clamored under her ribs.

"I wouldn't have to speak to you that way if you stopped acting like one." His voice was the hiss of a snake.

"I want to speak to Elliott and Ian." She forced a calm into her voice her insides couldn't match.

"No."

"Put them on the phone, or I'll come and get them." He couldn't stop her. She wasn't going to cave to him anymore. Until a judge said she couldn't have her children, she would not listen to him.

"Don't bother. We aren't at my house."

"What?" She stumbled.

"You heard me. I took them away for the weekend. I knew you would call and make me keep them until Monday so I decided a different location for the weekend would do us all good. I'll drop them at school Monday morning. You can retrieve them after school."

"Where are you?" Bile burned the back of her throat. He could be anywhere. Even out of the country. She took a deep breath, and reason seeped in. Not out of the country. The boys didn't have passports.

"Where we are is none of your business. They'll be returned on Monday."

"Don't you hurt them." She'd kill him.

"I love my children. What on earth would make you say something as horrible as that? But that's you. You're off the deep end again, and that's why my children will live with me permanently. You can't be trusted." He ended the call.

She screamed until her throat ached. The muscles in her neck spasmed. Her hands shook as she searched for Virginia's number. The voicemail picked up, and she yelled again.

"Please call me. David won't give me back the boys. I need help."

She poured a hefty glass of wine from the bottle Phoenix had brought yesterday. There had to be something she could use against David. He had to have a past before her. So why couldn't she find it?

She stopped with the wine glass at her lips. David hid things in a wall in his house. Ian mentioned it. If Ian had been right, whatever was behind that grate had been there when they were married. David hadn't wanted her to know about it while they were married. That only added up to no good. He must've forgotten about it because a safe or safe deposit box would make more sense.

She poured the wine down the drain, and she shoved her feet in her boots again. Grabbing her car keys, she yanked open the front door. Phoenix blocked her path.

"What are you doing here?" That came out harsher than she meant. She had a mission now and had to get to David's. If he was really away with the boys, now was her chance.

"I'm sorry. I got caught up at the firehouse. I screwed

up. I know. I promised I'd work on your house today. I'll start your projects tomorrow." He came in and closed the door. His limp seemed more pronounced than it did this morning. The smell of fresh air clung to him.

It took a second for her mind to register what he was talking about. "It's fine. You don't have to explain. I have to run out. Can I call you later?"

"Is everything okay?" The space between his brow creased.

"I have something I need to check on." She couldn't tell him what she was up to. He'd want to talk her out of it with his perfect town hero morals.

"Is it the bakery?"

"It's not that." He wasn't going to give up until she told him more details which she couldn't. He would change his opinion of her.

"Then what is it? You can tell me."

"No, Phoenix, I can't tell you. If I could tell you, I would. But this is personal and something I don't think you should be a part of." That wasn't true. Not any longer. They crossed the line of friendship into so much more. She didn't take what they'd done lightly, and guessed he hadn't either. Honesty was always the most important thing to him.

She glanced at the time. She needed to get to David's and see if there was anything hidden in one of those walls. David could come back any minute. He could be lying about being away. Maybe they were just at dinner. Or maybe they were returning tonight. Or maybe he had taken her children and run away. Her throat closed up more and more with each thought.

"Don't you think we're a little past hiding all our dark secrets?" The hurt in his eyes made her want to weep.

"I have to do this alone." She didn't know how to make him understand. These were her children and her responsibility. She did things by herself. Asking for help always backfired.

"You aren't alone anymore. I'm here. I'm not going anywhere. When are you going to trust me?"

"I don't have time for this right now. We can talk later. I'll call you." She avoided his gaze and tried to pass him.

He gripped her arm. She sucked in a breath, always worried a man's hand on her skin could be for harm. It was her knee jerk reaction. But this was Phoenix.

"Please, Mack, don't walk out on me. Not today." He released her and ran a hand over his face.

She hesitated. Something was wrong with her gentle giant, but she couldn't take the time to find out what it was. Later, when she knew what was in David's house. But she couldn't let him stand there and think she didn't want him. She wanted him so much it kept her up at night.

"This is going to sound crazy." She was really going to do this. If he left her when he heard, it was her own doing. She'd already asked him to keep them a secret. How much more could this man put up with?

"I don't mind a little crazy."

His smile was going to unhinge her. On a long breath, she told him her idea of going to David's and looking around. "I have the extra key. He never asked for it back."

"I'll go with you." He held out his hand.

"You're not going to talk me out of it?" She must've misheard him.

"Why would I do that? You want to go over to David's alone to snoop. I won't be able to talk you out of it unless I strip you out of your clothes and make mad love to you. That leaves me with going along in case something goes wrong."

"Did you just say make mad love?" She bit her lip not to laugh.

"What? Making love to me is funny?" He exaggerated the lift of his brow and the circle of his mouth.

"Anything but. I just never heard a guy talk like that."

"I hope I'm the last guy talking to you about making love to you." He dropped his gaze and shoved his hands in his pockets.

His words stunned her. She had been afraid all her issues would jinx any chance of something good happening between them. She had never had a whole lot of luck in relationships that mattered most. Even things between her and her sisters were often strained.

She put her hands on either side of his face, forcing him to meet her gaze. "You are very unexpected. Thank you for wanting to come with me. I'm less nervous when you're around."

"I like the sound of that." He placed a small kiss on her lips.

She would love to forget this stupid idea and rip his clothes off right in the living room. For a second, she wondered what it would be like to have him press her against the wall and take her standing.

"Let's go," she said.

~

MACK PARKED a couple of houses away from David's Victorian, the house that was once hers, and turned off the lights. She used to think the big house was beautiful. Now she hated it. The street was quiet. Most of the neighbors wouldn't be paying attention at this hour. They were the kind of people who only came out if there was a problem. Some of the houses were even empty until the summer season.

"What about security cameras?" Phoenix adjusted his brace.

"You can stay in the car. I don't want you to have to run if something goes wrong." A man bundled in a coat turned the corner with his tiny dog on a leash.

"Let me worry about me. Does he have cameras?"

"Phoenix, you're going to hurt yourself again the way you keep putting weight on that leg." The man went in the opposite direction. The coast was clear. They needed to go.

He leaned over and placed a warm kiss on her lips. "It's sweet the way you worry about me, but I can handle it. You're not answering my question. If your ex has security cameras around the house, he's going to see us on the footage."

"As far as I know, there aren't any."

"What about an alarm system?"

"I know the code. It's the boys' birthday." She reached for the door.

"Could he have changed it?" He grabbed her arm.

"Anything is possible. We'll have about thirty seconds

to get out of there and back to the car if the alarm sounds. Are you sure you don't want to wait for me here?" After the alarm sounded, if the code was changed, the police would arrive in minutes. Water Course didn't have a lot of crime. The police wouldn't waste time getting to the house.

She didn't want Phoenix to slow her down, but she did want his company.

"I can't protect you from inside the car. Why are you pushing me away?"

"I should be annoyed that you think I'm a damsel in distress, but the fact you want to be there for me is kind of sweet."

"I know you can take care of yourself. That doesn't change the fact that David has a height and weight advantage over you that I level off."

That he did. Phoenix was tall and strong. He could carry a hundred pounds of firefighter gear on his back. David was a bully. If David was home and saw them, he would think twice about getting aggressive with Phoenix around.

"Let's go. I can't wait any longer. I'm afraid I'm going to lose my mind."

She shivered against the cold wind and met Phoenix on the sidewalk. His smile warmed her insides. This amazing man wanted to be hers. She should trust him. No one else had tried to make her feel safe in her entire life except for Pop, and here was Phoenix taking this insane risk with her. He could jeopardize his entire career, and he hadn't even hesitated to come with her.

Their footsteps echoed against the cement. Her mind

yelled at her to turn around. This was a bad idea. She forced her legs to move forward. David's house was dark. The house to the left was also dark, and the first-floor shutters were closed. At least one set of neighbors wasn't home.

She held her head high and acted as if they belonged. Her stomach told a different story and braided like bread dough. Phoenix slipped his hand into hers and gave a squeeze.

"Thank you," she said.

They entered the house through the front door. The alarm began its hurried beeping. She swallowed the knot iced with fear in her throat. Her fingers shook over the keypad. She hit the wrong number and had to start again. Punching in six simple numbers would give her the time she needed to find evidence, if she would only get her act together. As she pressed the last digit, the alarm gave up its unsettling sounds.

"Nice," he said.

"I don't know which room Ian was in. Let's start with the master bedroom upstairs." She let out a long breath and unbuttoned her coat.

The moonlight streamed through the windows, creating enough light to make out objects. She hadn't been inside in over a year. That one fateful night she couldn't take the verbal abuse any longer and called Aria crying. Mack needed help to get the boys out of the house. Aria came at two in the morning with a baseball bat and told David to stay the hell away. Now all she wanted was for her boys to be safe. Just like that night.

The master bedroom was at the end of the hallway.

She looked inside the rooms along the way. Two rooms were designed for little boys. One painted light green with dragons and the other blue with shelves of books. Elliott and Ian. Tears caught her off guard and choked her.

Where were her sweet little boys? She took a step inside the green room and ran her fingers over the comforter. The space looked as if it had been in a magazine and not one lived in and loved by a child. Elliott's room at home had stuffed animals piled up in the corner. They had made a tent out of a sheet for him to play Legos in. No Legos were anywhere in this room.

"Hey, I know this is hard, but we need to keep moving." Phoenix leaned in and whispered in her ear.

His warmth and strong presence gave her the courage to step out into the hallway. She was doing this for the boys. She needed to pull herself together. "You're right."

The door to the master bedroom was open, and the room was tidy the way David liked it. No clothes sat in baskets on the floor. The four window shades were raised to the exact height. Nothing decorated any of the dresser tops. David didn't want personal items left out. He always yelled when she left a book by her bedside lamp. He would remove picture frames she had left on her dresser and shove them in drawers.

"Which wall?" Phoenix turned, taking in the room.

"The one with the heating duct. It might be by his tall dresser. I don't remember."

Phoenix wandered in one direction while she went in the other.

"It's here." He squatted down with his bad leg straight out and shined a tiny flashlight into the duct. "Empty."

"We could be searching for a long time. There's too many rooms in this dumb house."

"The best hiding places are in plain sight. Does he have an office? Would Ian have been playing in there?"

"David used a small room on the first floor as an office back when we were together. Ian might've been in there." Might've been nice if she had asked.

They headed back down. Moving light splashed across the wall. She gripped Phoenix's shoulder. "Someone's coming."

"I think it's just a car going down the street." He took her hand.

"What if it's David?" Icy dread froze her stomach.

"Then we'd better get the hell out of here."

"But I didn't find what I came for." She couldn't leave without the proof she needed. This was her only chance.

"Let me check the road. Stay here." He limped out of the foyer into the front room where the windows faced the street.

She held her breath. He was hurting. She should never have let him come, and would make it up to him somehow. He returned with a smile.

"Like I said, just a car driving by. Let's look in that office then go. I don't want to risk him coming back while we're here."

"Okay. This was a crazy idea." Her craziest idea ever.

"No worse than some. Lead the way."

She turned away from the staircase and followed the small hallway. David's office was mostly an ornate wood desk with scrolled legs. The top was empty and clean except for a closed laptop. He had a guest chair that matched the leather tufted executive chair behind the desk. Nothing hung on the light-colored walls. A small filing cabinet was tucked into a cut out in the wall.

"How fucking uptight is this guy?" Phoenix said.

Heat burned her cheeks. By bringing Phoenix, she had allowed him to see her mistakes through a magnifying glass.

"I was young and stupid."

"Hey, this has nothing to do with you. Not his choices, his behavior, or this shit about him trying to take the kids." He put his hands on her shoulders and held her gaze.

"I married him."

"We all make mistakes. Give yourself a break. Start looking."

"I'll do it. Just go out into the hallway and watch for more lights."

"Are you sure?"

"Yes. I don't want you getting up and down. It's a small room. Now go."

He handed her the tiny screwdriver and went out into the hall. She dropped to her knees and began looking. The first heating duct was secure in place. She pointed the flashlight inside. Nothing. Maybe Ian had seen incorrectly. But he was the child who paid attention to the little details, even at five.

Her heart pounded in her ears. She was running out of options. Kneeling down at the other grate in the room, she wiggled the metal. It rattled and sent a shiver over her skin. With the tiny screwdriver, she loosened the screws further. The plate fell forward and clanked on the floor. The noise reverberated in the air. She checked over her shoulder for Phoenix, but the doorway remained empty.

She took a deep breath and pointed the light into the vent. A small brown box, no bigger than a cigar box, was just inside the opening. Her hands shook as she pulled it toward her. Many questions assaulted her. The inside of this thing could be all the answers or more questions.

She lifted the lid and held the flashlight at an angle so she could see inside. Nothing made sense. A birth certificate of a boy named David Hubert born on the date she knew to be David's birthday. The parents on the birth certificate were not the names on the gravesites he had shown her.

There was also a death certificate of the same boy belonging to the same set of parents. The death certificate was dated two years after the boy David was born. David Hubert had died in California at the age of two. A California driver's license was issued to David Hubert only a year before she met David with the picture of the man she'd once called her husband.

Her mind couldn't catch up to what her eyes were seeing. She stared at the documents as if she floated from above. David had told her he was from Connecticut. He had said he'd never been to California because she wanted to go on a trip there, and he talked her out of it. He said nothing good ever happened in California. She had thought he was joking.

He had been lying to her all this time. He wasn't David Hubert. Then who was he? And where was he with her children? Panic gripped her like a snake around her neck. Her head spun. She tried to call out to Phoenix, but her voice stuck.

"Mack, did you find anything?" His voice was a buoy in the ocean for her to grasp.

She held up the box with trembling hands.

"Holy shit. Take pictures."

"What?"

"Take pictures. You can't take this with you. He can't know you were here. Send the pictures to your lawyer. Have her hire a private investigator. Hurry, Mack, do it."

His sense seemed to shake some of the fog away. She fumbled for her phone and opened the camera app. With shaking hands, she took several pictures.

"Let's get out of here." She put the box back and the grate into place.

They hurried through the house. She reset the alarm and locked the door. The cold air shook her fully awake. She had married a liar. She had slept with a man who had pretended to be someone he wasn't. The father of her children had stolen the identity of an innocent person taken from this world before his time. It was unfathomable, and yet she had the proof on her phone.

"I'll drive." Phoenix took her keys.

She didn't argue.

CHAPTER TWELVE

$\mathcal{M}$ ack shifted from one foot to the other. Her stomach had been tied up in a tight weave all day. School would let out in two minutes. She had called earlier to make sure the boys were there. The office secretary thought she was out of her mind, but Mack didn't care. David had brought them back as promised. She saw no sign of him now. He might be backing off for a few days, with the court date so close. It was wishful thinking. She had been up all night worried the police would show up at her door for breaking and entering. When the sun came up, and no one had knocked on her door to read her her rights she breathed a long sigh of peace.

She had emailed those pictures to Virginia as soon as Phoenix brought her home after they left David's. Her lawyer would have the resources to get to the bottom of this mess, and she'd be able to win against David. Finally. Her luck had turned. She deserved a break as much as the next person. She'd spend the rest of her life paying Virginia off, but it would be worth it.

Phoenix had called her three times while she had been at work and too unfocused to take his call or help her customers. She had let his calls land in voicemail. After she saw her boys, she'd call him back.

She was grateful for all that he had done for her. She had shown him exactly how grateful in the early hours of Sunday morning. She was falling hard for him, but right now she needed to get to the end of this nightmare. Today was about being with her boys and waiting for Virginia to tell her some good news. Only then could she breathe with ease and even tell Aria and Hawk about her and Phoenix. She'd shout it from the top of the school.

The bell rang. Children in all shapes and sizes in coats the color of sprinkles scattered out of the glass doors filled with the innocent joy only a child can know. Teachers with walkie talkies shouted orders. The buses waited to gobble up the students and take them home.

She had asked Mrs. Zaggler to bring the boys out to her. She couldn't handle going inside the building and faking it for the other mothers living their simple little lives. Her life had never been simple. Maybe it could be soon.

Her heart skipped a beat. Elliott and Ian came out holding Mrs. Zaggler's hands. Elliott skipped while Ian moved in more of a march. She fought her legs to keep from running to them.

But Elliott saved her. "Mommy." He tore free of his teacher and jumped into her arms.

She hugged him close. "Hey, buddy." His little body

snuggled against hers. His sweet smell clung to him. Love burst her chest open.

She opened her other arm for Ian who stepped into her hug.

"Hi, Mommy," Ian said with his serious little voice.

She kissed the top of Ian's head.

"I missed you both so much. Thank you, Mrs. Zaggler." She hugged the boys again.

"My pleasure. The boys had great days. Remember to do your spelling homework, boys." She waved and went back toward the school.

"Let's go home. I want to hear all about your weekend away." She drank in the sounds of their voices replaying all the fun they had with David.

It should have been her taking them to the indoor water park and the zoo. She had to push the growing jealousy away because she didn't want to miss any piece of information she could use for her case. But the boys seemed happy and fine. David had taken care of them and held up his end of the deal and delivered them to school. He was good at playing this game, but maybe she had put a kink in his plan. She wasn't the one with an unexplained identity.

Her phone vibrated in her pocket. If she hadn't been waiting for Virginia, she would've let it go. She eased her hand out of Ian's. "Mommy has to answer this call."

Virginia's name appeared on the screen. She hit the green button twice before the call connected.

"Virginia, what did you find out?"

"Mack, did you break into David's house?" Virginia's voice was cold as steal.

"What?" She had heard just fine. Her mind needed to stall Virginia in order to find an answer.

"Did you break in? How did you get into the house?"

"Who said I was in his house?" She ushered the boys to the car and helped them in the back. She didn't want them to hear any of this conversation.

"Don't bother. I know. How did you get in?"

"I used the key." The truth burst out before she could stop it. She had never been good at lying.

"You still have a key?"

"Yes, Virginia. What's the matter?" Besides the fact she was busted.

"David is pressing charges against you. For trespassing. He had security cameras in the house that caught you walking around when he wasn't home. His lawyer called me as a courtesy to give me a heads-up. Everything you found is going to end up not being useful."

"But how? He's not who he said he is."

"Let's hope the PI can find something we can use. I can misdirect the way we got the idea to check on him. But none of that matters. I need you to meet me down at the police station right now. I'll take care of this. And who's the man with you?"

"The police station? I can't go there. I have the boys."

"If you don't meet me there now, the police will show up at your house in an hour and take you down in handcuffs. Is that what you want? Call your sister and tell her to meet you there too. She'll have to take the boys, or David will come for them."

"Not David."

"And the man, Mack? Who was with you? He's going to be arrested too."

"He can't be arrested. This isn't about him. I made him do it." She couldn't allow Phoenix to be hurt too. He would lose everything because of her.

"It's not up to you. The police are going to use facial recognition. If he's anywhere in the system, they'll find him."

"It's Phoenix Egan."

"The hero firefighter? Oh, please don't tell me you're seeing him. Not after I told you not to get involved with anyone right now. You're handing David those kids. Call your boyfriend and tell him to head down. I'll be waiting for you both. I can represent him too. We'll go in together." Virginia ended the call.

She leaned against the car and put her head between her knees. Her life was over. She couldn't be arrested. David would win. They wouldn't be able to prove he was lying.

She needed to think. How could she get out of this? Could she run? Pack up everything she could and take the boys anywhere from here? She couldn't pull that off. She couldn't spend her life hiding.

With a deep breath, she called Aria.

"Hey, Mack."

"I need your help."

PHOENIX CHECKED HIS PHONE AGAIN. Mack had ignored all his calls today. He couldn't figure out what was going on.

They had been fine yesterday. Heat burned his core remembering how fine they were in her bed.

She had been freaked out about what she'd found at her ex's place. He didn't blame her. He was a little weirded out too. David had a secret identity. Who was the fucker? What was the guy running from? And what else had he done that might hurt Mack and the boys?

He took the beer from Hawk. "Thanks."

"When do you come back to work?" Hawk dropped onto the sofa. The cushions gave way with a whoosh.

Phoenix had come to Hawk and Aria's for dinner. He didn't want to be alone, and he didn't want to be at Mack's when she came back with the boys. She needed time with them. The pain of missing them and worrying David wouldn't come back with them had haunted her.

He had worked on her house during the day, but made sure he was gone before she could get back. If she had answered one text, he might've stayed to see her, but her silence said more than her words. The clock reminded him school should have let out. She would be home about now. He missed her and wished she would at least reach out to him.

"Yo, Phoenix. Did you even hear the last thing I said?" Hawk tossed a napkin at him.

"What was it again?"

"When are you coming back to the firehouse? Timmy wants dibs on your bunk."

"Timmy can go fuck himself. I earned that spot." He turned the beer in his hand, avoiding Hawk's gaze. "The chief wants me on the schedule next week."

He wasn't sure if he was ready yet. He wished he had

told Mack about his concerns while they were in bed, but she had so much on her mind. She didn't need more to think about. He could manage his emotions. Or quit his job. Could he tell Hawk what he was thinking? Isn't that what they learned in grief counseling? Except this was different. This time it was him.

"Hey, there's something I could use advice on." He peeled the label on the bottle.

"What's that—"

"Okay, we'll be right down. Don't panic." Aria hurried into the room on the phone and waving her hand. "He's here. No, no, no. I'll tell him. Drive safely." She hit the screen on the phone and stared at them with wide eyes.

Hawk jumped to his feet. "What's the matter?"

"Mack's being arrested for trespassing. We have to get to the police station to take the boys."

Phoenix dropped the beer. The foam spilled out of the neck and onto the floor. "Please tell me this is a joke."

She ran out of the room and back with a towel. "You're being arrested too, but you're getting the chance to turn yourself in. What the hell did you two do?"

Hawk shoved him. "What the fuck is going on, Phoenix?"

He ran a hand over his face. This was bad. He knew some guys he could call in a favor with. He wouldn't let Mack get arrested. She would lose her kids.

"It's a long story. I need to get to her," he said.

"No, you're going to tell me what's going on. We're family. This could affect your job. Our construction business. No fucking secrets. That's our rule." Hawk stood in his path.

"We went to her ex's house to find something to use against him. She had the key. We let ourselves in."

"Why would you do that? You know that's against the law," Hawk said.

"Because she needed my help, and I love her."

"Excuse me?" Aria's mouth hung open.

"I'm in love with your sister. I have been for a while, but it's only been the past few weeks we've been seeing each other as more than friends." Mack was going to kill him for telling their secret, but he didn't want to hide anymore. He could help her better if everyone knew what was at stake.

"And no one told us?" Aria threw her arms in the air.

"She wanted it to be kept quiet because of the custody battle. She didn't want David to have anything to hold against her."

"So, you go into his house when he isn't home?" Hawk shook his head. "This is by far your biggest screw up."

"Not now, Hawk," he said.

"Let's go. We can talk about your and my sister's betrayal later. We can't leave her alone," Aria said.

"Do you think it's a good idea for you to be there?" Hawk went to Aria and put a hand on her belly.

Aria slapped his hand away. "Hawk Egan, I love you, but you will have to tie me to a metal post if you think I'm not going to help my sister now. I'm pregnant. Not an invalid. Get your coat and get out of my way."

"She told you." He brushed past Hawk.

"Shut up." Hawk slapped him on the back of his head.

CHAPTER THIRTEEN

*M*ack waited down the street from the police station. Her hands were sweating. She had to force the bile back down her throat. She couldn't get arrested.

"Mommy, when are we going home?" Elliott whined in the back. Ian rubbed his eyes.

Her heart broke. She had let her boys down. What kind of mother risks getting arrested? Even the possibility of David lying about his real identity wasn't making her feel any better.

"Soon. Aunt Aria is coming to get you."

"I don't want Aunt Aria. I want to go home with you," Elliott said.

She let out a long breath. Virginia pulled into the parking lot of the police station. Mack checked her mirrors. No sign of Aria yet. She had promised to tell Phoenix they wanted him too. He was going to lose his job because of her. Not only was she a terrible mother, she was a terrible person.

"Mommy, I'm hungry," Ian said.

"Hang on a few more minutes."

She couldn't pull into that lot until Aria showed up. Her phone started buzzing. She wanted to ignore it, but Virginia would only keep calling back.

"I'm almost there." What was one more lie?

"I'm at the station. I'll wait in my car until you get here. Is your sister coming?"

Aria's car whizzed into the lot next to Virginia's. Aria, Hawk, and Phoenix piled out.

She put the car in drive and followed them in. Phoenix turned at the sound of her car approaching. His smile gave her the strength to get out of the car. She wanted to run into his arms, but resisted. Confessing their relationship now would only make matters worse. She could explain his presence in David's house as her friend. Everyone knew they were friends.

Phoenix cleared the space as if his knee had never bothered him. He gathered her in his arms and kissed her head. She tried to ease out of his embrace.

"Don't bother. He told us." Aria saddled up to their side.

"You told? Why?"

"Because there's no point hiding."

"Okay, folks. We need to get inside. Mack and Phoenix, you come with me. Aria and Hawk, please take those children home and get them a warm meal. We'll get this over as quickly as possible." Virginia waved her arms to direct their traffic.

Another vehicle pulled into the lot. The mayor jumped

out of his import. He hustled over and shook hands with Phoenix and Hawk.

"What's going on?" She gripped Phoenix's arm.

"The mayor owes me a favor. It's going to be okay, babe," Phoenix said.

"Virginia, do you mind if I accompany you?" the mayor said.

"Alex, if it gets me home in time for my favorite show, you can do whatever you want." Virginia hooked her arm through the mayor's.

"Boys, give me a hug. Be good for Aunt Aria and Uncle Hawk." She gripped her boys.

"It's going to be fine." Aria peeled her away from the kids. "Go with Phoenix. And Mack, it's okay if you love him. You deserve to be happy."

GOOD NEWS. Bad news. Mack hated that expression. It was as if the good news wasn't allowed to hang around for very long. Phoenix held the door for her. She stepped outside. The police station parking lot was dimly lit by a couple of lights. The cold air cooled her heated cheeks. She gulped it down, hoping to still her nerves.

"Can I get a ride from you?" He slid his hand into hers.

She pulled away and marched to her car. "Why did you tell them about us?"

He followed. "Us being together is not a big deal."

"Really? David will use it against me."

"Mack, get serious. David has us on video in his house uninvited. That's what he's using."

"Having a boyfriend is just one more thing he can say that makes me a bad mother."

"What are you saying? I'm no good for your kids?"

She didn't know what she was saying. Her head still reeled from what just happened. If it hadn't been for the mayor, she would be in a jail cell and so would Phoenix. He didn't seem the least bit affected about what just happened, but then again, he had nothing to lose. The town hero could do no wrong.

"I can't have this conversation now. I want to go home to my children before I lose them for good." The mayor was able to have any charges removed, but David was still in his right to show the video to the judge overseeing the custody case.

She and Phoenix had broken the law, and David had the proof. She would never win if Virginia couldn't find a way to prove David was lying about who he was before they went to court. Right now, he could argue she made it all up. Doctored the photos. And with the proof she'd broken into his house, along with his lies about her ability to be a sound mother, she couldn't win.

"Let me come home with you. I'll help you make dinner. You don't have to do it all alone," he said.

"No. I'll drop you back at Aria's since I have to get Elliott and Ian, but that's it. We're through."

"Mack, you can't mean that. You're upset about today. I get that, but we're good together."

"No, Phoenix, we're good in bed. We might've been good friends, but I have to worry about myself and my children. I tried to tell you that, but I never trust myself when it comes to men. I always let myself be persuaded into doing something I don't really want."

"You didn't want to be with me? Are you saying you felt forced?" His face twisted with hurt.

Her heart screamed to stop. She was saying stupid things. But she had gone too far with him. It was all her fault. She should've toed the line, and David wouldn't have threatened to take the boys away. She had done this. She deserved what was happening. She certainly didn't deserve Phoenix.

"Mack, for Christ's sake, I'm not your ex-husband. Don't you know that by now? Have I ever given you any reason to believe I would try and make you do something you didn't want to do?" His face turned red.

"It's not you. You've been perfect. More than perfect. I'm just not good at this. Go find someone else to make you happy. It can't be me."

He rubbed his eye with the heel of his hand. The red blotches deepened on his face. He cursed and turned away from her.

Her breath caught. He couldn't possibly be. Not the man who was afraid of nothing. The man who ran into a burning school and saved a classroom of children without a thought for himself.

"Phoenix, I—" She tried to take step toward him.

"Stop. I've heard enough."

"Please, let me explain." She was afraid. She wasn't fearless like him. She needed more time. She didn't want him to look at her as if he'd never seen her before.

"Save it. You don't need to try and spare my feelings. It's always been whatever you wanted from me. I never wanted to push you, but I had been stupid enough to think you'd fall for me." He turned on his heel.

"Where are you going?"

"Back to Hawk's to get my truck." He kept going.

"Let me take you. You'll hurt your knee." She called after his back.

"I'd rather walk." He didn't turn around.

He kept going until the dark street swallowed him up, and she stood there all alone.

CHAPTER FOURTEEN

*P*hoenix buttoned his fire coat and grabbed his helmet. He could do this. It was just the stupid parade. Only his lungs didn't seem to know that. He struggled to take a deep breath. This was pathetic. He'd been a firefighter most of his adult life, and now he couldn't do his fucking job.

"Egan, let's go," the chief called from the front of the house.

"Coming." He took his spot in the jump seat opposite Hawk.

"You still haven't spoken to her," Hawk said.

"It doesn't matter. It's over." The fight with Mack last week still had him reeling. He had hoped she would call or text. But she had remained silent. He didn't understand how she could throw away what they had so easily. Even their friendship. He missed talking to her. He wanted to go into the bakery to get a coffee like he had a million times before, but she had made herself clear.

"It looks like what happened matters. Your face is all

twisted up. Are you going to puke?" Hawk had to raise his voice over the noise of the wind.

Phoenix tried not to hit him. Losing Mack only made what was happening while he sat on this truck worse. He'd have to find a way to get over it. Now.

Merle pulled the ladder truck into the parade line. People filled the street, cheering and clapping. The sky was dark gray. They hadn't seen the sun in days. Fog left a layer of salty wetness on everything. The raw weather matched his mood.

The parade route was two miles. That's all he had to get through. He wasn't officially on the schedule until the end of the week. A few more days would be all he needed. That's what he had been telling himself. He ran a hand over his face. His fears made him sick to his stomach.

The truck eased forward. Merle turned on the lights and sirens. Kids jumped up and down. Adults waved. Someone shouted, "thank you, Phoenix."

He scanned the crowd as they crawled along. Many people he knew waved from the sides. The one person he wanted to see wasn't there. She could be in the back of the crowd, but his gut told him she hadn't shown. He hoped the boys would ask to go to the parade, and she'd cave for them.

The truck made a right turn for the last leg of the parade. Aria waved and yelled for Hawk. She put her fingers to her lips and whistled. Hawk leaned over and shouted back.

If Mack were there, this would be where she'd stand. Aria squatted down and pointed. Elliott waved with fury. A slice of hope pricked his chest as his gaze searched the people standing in hats and coats. Some drank from Styrofoam cups. Some clapped. None of them were Mack.

Mack's other sister, Liv, stepped off the sidewalk and lifted Ian so he could see too. He swallowed the disappointment like a sour pill. Mack must've called Liv home to help her when he had been more than willing to be the support in her life.

Ian waved. He returned the gesture not sure if the boys even saw him, but wanted them to notice. He missed them too. He sank back in his seat. His stomach burned long and hard.

The rest of the parade passed by in a fog. He barely noticed Merle parking the truck at the end of the route. The mayor expected him to say a few words since he had bailed him and Mack out. He jumped out of the truck and made his way to the podium.

"The mayor will introduce you first. Just speak in your regular voice. The microphone will pick you up," the mayor's assistant said.

He didn't have a speech planned. He was just going to shake Alex's hand and get off the stage as fast as possible.

"Phoenix, wait." Hawk ran toward him. "We got a call. You might as well come. You're suited up, and we need the hands. It's a four-alarm and burning fast."

Hawk didn't wait. He turned and ran.

"I'm sorry. Duty calls. Please apology to Alex for me." He followed his brother because Hawk expected him to. And any other time he would have without hesitation. Someone was in trouble and needed him.

He couldn't let them down too.

~

THE TRUCK PULLED up as close to the house as it could get. A townhouse on the end had caught fire because of faulty wiring. Electric fires spread quickly. The flames had busted through the roof and licked the unit next to it.

His team hustled. Everyone did their job. No one needed to be told what to do, which was primarily his job. They had trained, perfected, and performed these duties a million times. He could do it in his sleep.

But his heart rate climbed, and his breathing labored. He was sweating, and he hadn't even stepped inside.

What if he couldn't find his way out? What if he froze? His hands shook. He dropped the tools on the street. They scattered and rolled.

"Phoenix, what the fuck?" Hawk shouted.

"I don't know." He stared at his hands as if he had never seen them before.

Timmy handed him back the tools.

"Thanks, man."

"Sure thing." Timmy adjusted his hat.

"Get your mask," Hawk said directly to him. "We need to go in. There's a spot in the back we can break through. Timmy and Merle will have the hose. We're lucky. Everyone is out. But we need to hurry before the entire complex goes up. The wind just shifted off the ocean."

He and Hawk were the best trained. Merle was getting too old to go into buildings. His bulk was better used holding the hose down.

He wiped the sweat from his eyes. His legs grew too

heavy to move. Fear reached down his throat and took hold. His mouth went dry. Hawk's face blurred.

"Are you going to be sick?" Hawk gripped his shoulder.

"I can't go in." He handed the tools to Hawk.

"What do you mean you can't go in?"

"I can't. I can't go inside that house. If I do, someone could die. I can't take that chance. Take Timmy. I'll run the hose with Merle."

Hawk glanced over his shoulder at the burning structure. "This isn't over. We'll talk about it later. Tim, with me."

"But I've got the hose." Timmy held up the hose as if that would explain everything.

"Now. Get your mask. Phoenix will work with Merle." Hawk's harsh words sent Timmy running.

"Thank you." Speaking hurt his throat as if he'd already been inside that building. He struggled to keep Hawk's gaze.

"Don't thank me just yet." Hawk ran off with Timmy on his heels.

Merle gripped his arm. "That incident at the school screwed with you. Hang it up, young man. Before you end up dead. Or worse, someone else does."

CHAPTER FIFTEEN

*P*hoenix needed a shower. He stunk like sweat and smoke. It had taken an hour to put out the fire. They weren't able to save the townhouse. The owner would need to rebuild, but they did save the unit next door. The call had been a success. Except for him.

Merle didn't say another word to him. Tim was the only one who didn't seem to realize what had happened. Hawk shot him glares. His brother would want answers, and he deserved them. Phoenix just hadn't been honest with anyone. A firehouse can't be run that way. Lives were on the line.

He cleared out his locker and shoved everything into a duffel. With his keys gripped in his fist, he found the chief at his desk.

"Do you have a second, sir?" He knocked on the open door.

"Have a seat, Egan." Chief Wylie pointed to the only other chair in the room.

"I think I'll stand, thanks." He kept his shoulders straight and met the chief's gaze. "I'm resigning."

"Like that?" Chief cocked an eyebrow.

"You know what happened today. I can't take the chance I'm going to get someone killed." Which could've happened if he were the only man able to get inside that structure.

"Did you go to the therapist?"

"I thought I had it under control." He had allowed his arrogance to get in the way. He had also made the mistake that his time with Mack would heal whatever had ailed him.

"Take a leave of absence. Come back in a few months after you really worked through it."

"I'm an embarrassment. The guys can't trust me. I don't trust myself. I'll fill out whatever paperwork you need me to, but I'm done." The honesty hurt to admit, but it had to be done.

"Firefighting isn't just what you do. It's who you are. What are you going to do if you don't do that?" Chief leaned back in his seat and steepled his fingers over his large stomach.

"Hawk and I have the construction business. I'll do that full time." If his brother would ever talk to him again.

"Have you spoken to your brother about this problem of yours?"

"He's not talking to me right now."

"It's only been a couple of hours. Give him time. He isn't going to want to be here without you."

He shook his head and laughed. "I doubt that."

"After Wyatt died and Hawk pulled himself together,

he told me the reason he could come to work every day was because you were here. He needed you."

"Yeah, well, that was a long time ago now. Now he has Aria and a baby on the way. Hawk has his life back. He doesn't need me here to watch out for him. He'll be better off not having me here and worrying I'll freeze when he needs me most. I couldn't live with letting him down." He was the older brother. It was his job to take care of Hawk, not the other way around.

After Wyatt died, Phoenix had to be the man of the family. He couldn't be a man if he couldn't do his job with confidence.

"Whatever you say, Egan. It's your choice. I'll email you the forms for resignation. If you need a reference, I'll be glad to do it. And if you ever change your mind, you will always have a place here. We're your family."

"Thanks." He hurried from the firehouse, fighting back the emotions threatening to take over.

The pain in his chest from losing his job and losing Mack in the same week was too much to bear. He needed a drink. And to forget.

PHOENIX PULLED into the parking lot of the Tip of My Tongue bar. He stared at his hands on the steering wheel. If he couldn't be a firefighter, he didn't know who he was. His entire life had been about the job from when he was a kid. It was simply understood he and his brothers would follow in their father's footsteps, and he had wanted to. Being a firefighter was the only redeemable quality their father had. Until he dishonored the job.

Phoenix had wanted to be better than his father. He wanted to be the man his father never was. Wyatt had already been on that road. Everyone had respected Wyatt, including him and Hawk. When Wyatt had died, the void in his life was a chasm. He had to become the brother who carried the honor of the job on his shoulders with pride. Hawk had fallen apart because he believed Wyatt's death was his fault. Phoenix hadn't had the luxury of losing his shit too. How ironic it was happening to him now. He thought he was invincible. He was very wrong.

He slid out of the truck and banged his knee. His insides burned with anger. If anyone even looked at him the wrong way before he was so drunk he couldn't drive home, he would start a fight. He didn't care anymore. He was tired of being the town hero. He had more of his father in him than he ever admitted.

The inside of the bar was dark with its low ceilings and paneled walls. The lights were kept at the level of dim. The drinks were usually strong and the conversation light this time of year when the year-rounders didn't go out much on a cold weeknight. In the summer, this place would be wall-to-wall people either bumping and grinding on the dance floor or three deep at the bar.

The stool at the end of the bar was empty. He slid on and signaled to Alicia who poured a beer from the tap for some guy and his girl. She gave him the one-minute sign. With his back to the bathrooms, he could see the front door and most of the seats. The stage was empty tonight.

He was grateful there wouldn't be any bass pounding in his head.

Alicia came over and leaned forward on the bar with her hands. Probably out of habit more than the fact she couldn't hear him tonight. The place held a hush over it. Music piped in from the jukebox. Some old Michael McDonald song.

"What can I get you, Phoenix?" Alicia's hair was tied in a small knot on the top of her head. She wore a black headband over her hair too. A bronze heart swung from a black necklace at the base of her neck.

"A Stella. Thanks." He handed over his keys.

She raised an eyebrow but didn't reach for them.

"I'm walking home tonight." When she wouldn't take his keys, he pushed them toward her.

"Rough day?"

"I've seen better." He looked away. He needed her to go get his drink and not ask any more questions.

"Maybe you need a friend tonight instead of getting drunk."

"I'm not sure which friends I can count on tonight." The person he wanted most was done with him.

She had said he forced her. Well, not forced. Convinced was a better word. Her feelings had not been real. All those nights in bed with him, when she called out his name, he believed she wanted to be there. He needed to punch something.

"I can be someone you can count on tonight, Phoenix. I don't want you doing anything stupid. I'll be right back." Alicia grabbed his keys and sashayed away.

She was petite. He could probably throw her over his

STACEY WILK

shoulder with one hand. Which he might do in a fire, but he would no longer be in a fire situation. Her jeans hugged her tiny ass and her thin legs.

She placed the glass down on a napkin and opened the bottle. The beer was golden with a small foam on top. She flashed a high voltage smile and bit her bottom lip. It wouldn't be much of a stretch to get Alicia to come home with him. They had flirted before. Even back in high school, but he had never been interested in Alicia. He would never take Alicia home even if it was her idea. He wanted Mack's curves pressed against him.

He downed half the beer.

She left him alone except to refill his beer three times. He sank into the buzz that was starting to take effect. His head was fuzzy like he was in a washing machine, but not enough to push Mack out of the front of his mind. What had her lawyer said about the identification they had found? Could that prove anything? She deserved to win that case. He had wanted to be there with her when the verdict was handed out. She would fall apart if things went against her. He wanted to be the man she could count on. He drank more and signaled for two more.

Two guys played pool in the corner under a swinging light. They were young. Probably still in college. They laughed and shoved each other without a care in the world. He drank and watched.

He had been like those guys once. Young. Afraid of nothing. Today had scared the shit out of him and reminded him of his mortality. He couldn't stand himself at the moment. He was like rotting food left out in the heat. The beer wasn't making him forget, so he drank more.

He slid from the stool. The floor slipped out from under him, and his feet tangled. He caught himself before he clocked his chin on the bar. He finished his beer, left fifty bucks under his glass, and walked toward the pool table.

The door opened, and the cold air whisked in and slapped him in the face. His head cleared for a second before it went fuzzy again. Hawk stood in the doorway. His lip curled in a snarl. Their gazes met.

"What are you doing here?" Phoenix said.

"Looking for you." Hawk unzipped his jacket.

"Leave me alone." He didn't need to hear whatever it was Hawk was about to say. He could guess how things would go. And Hawk would be right.

"We need to talk. Let's grab a booth. I'll buy you a beer." Hawk pointed at an empty booth, but Phoenix didn't budge.

"I've had plenty to drink." Too much, in fact. He would regret it in the morning.

He stole a glance at the guys by the pool table. They had taken their drinks and found a spot in the corner. He'd missed his chance to prove to himself he wasn't washed up. The empty pool table didn't hold the same appeal it had only moments ago. He had wanted to fight with someone. Just not Hawk.

"Then let me drive you home," Hawk said.

"I'm not ready to go home."

"Then I guess I'm staying until you are."

"You shouldn't be at a bar." That was the right thing to

say. He could still be the big brother even when his life didn't make sense.

"Don't worry about me. I can handle myself."

"It must feel pretty good to be the brother on top, huh? You can finally look down your nose at me. I'm the fuckup, right? You've got your life all straightened out now. I don't need your pity."

"I'm not here to pity you or judge you. You're my brother, and you're hurting. I know I was mad earlier today, but I want to help you. Let's get a booth before you make a scene." Hawk tried to grab his arm, but he yanked it away.

"I don't give a shit about a scene." And he couldn't bear to have Hawk give him the speech he'd given so many times. He wanted to stay mad because mad made sense.

"You should. People are watching you."

Faces pointed in their direction. Someone held up their phone. His vision blurred more. The temperature in the room climbed. He lunged for the person with the phone. His hand grasped it, but his fingers slipped. He landed on the table and sent their glasses to the floor. A loud crash silenced the rest of the room.

Hawk grabbed him by his shirt and hoisted him to his feet. "I'm sorry for my brother's behavior. I'll pay for your drinks," he said to the couple at the table.

"I'm not." He tried to pry himself free of his brother's grasp.

"He's drunk, and a bit of an asshole." Hawk let him go, but kept a hand on his shoulder.

"You don't need to speak for me."

"Phoenix, maybe it's time for you to go," Alicia said from the bar. "I have his keys, Hawk."

Hawk held up a hand, and Alicia tossed them. She crossed her arms over her chest and nodded in the direction of the door.

"I'll take you home," Hawk said.

"I said I wasn't going home." There was nothing there for him. He wouldn't be able to stand the quiet house or the wail of the wind against the windows. He'd think about Mack and how he didn't have a job anymore. "I'm going to have another beer."

"Alicia isn't going to serve you."

"I left her a big tip. She'll serve me."

"Will you shut up and come with me? You're acting like a damn child. Get over yourself. You're not the first guy to come back to work and have a problem. It doesn't make you weak."

He shoved Hawk. Hawk backed up a few steps, but his drunken move did little to budge his brother who was the most physically fit in their department and not suffering the disadvantage of being drunk. The snarl returned to Hawk's face, and his fists clenched. Phoenix took a ready stand because Hawk wanted to punch him like when they were kids.

"You don't want to start a fight, Phoenix."

That's exactly what he wanted. He shoved Hawk again.

"Take it outside, guys." Alicia held a bat over her shoulder. For a tiny thing, she was tough.

Hawk turned and pushed through the door. Phoenix stole a glance at Alicia. She showed him the bat and pointed at the door. He followed his brother.

Hawk waited by his truck. His new truck that never broke down because Hawk was always practical.

"Go home, baby brother. I don't need you." He tripped on the gravel in the parking lot.

"Get in the truck, or I will drag your ass into it, and I don't want to do that. I want to go home and be with my wife who isn't a gigantic pain in the butt."

"You have the perfect life, don't you? It always works out for you. No matter what trouble you find yourself in, you slip out of it." Words he would never say were working their way too close to his mouth. It was the booze and the pain. He didn't want to hurt alone.

Hawk pushed off the truck and took a step closer. His eyes narrowed. "What are you getting at?"

"You fuck up your life royally, and you end up with your job waiting for you. You even get yourself promoted. Aria took you back after what you did to her. You're the fucking king of the hill, aren't you?"

Hawk cleared the space between them in a flash. They stood nose to nose. Hawk's hot breath was on his face.

"Shut the fuck up." Hawk poked his chest.

He should stop while he still could. He'd be sober by the time he walked home. This fight didn't need to happen, but deep down he had thought those things about Hawk. He knew it wasn't really his fault that Wyatt died, but it had been Hawk's screwup that had Wyatt on that floor that broke loose and sent him into the basement on his back. He'd lost his big brother too and wanted to be mad at someone for it. Most days he could push the feelings aside, but not tonight after he lost everything else that had meant so much.

"Why should I? It's true, isn't it? You barely broke stride after Wyatt died."

Hawk's fist collided with his gut. The pain shot up his stomach and his back, shaking him to the core. The beer tried to come back up, but he clamped his mouth shut on the grunt in his throat. He toppled forward and landed on his shoulder. Gravel jumped up and bit his cheek.

"I know you're talking shit because you're drunk and mad, but if you ever say something like that to me again, I'll beat the shit out of you." Hawk got into his truck and drove away.

Phoenix pushed off the ground and waited for the world to stop spinning. His knee throbbed. His shoulder complained. Gulping in cold air only managed to make his stomach hurt worse. He deserved what Hawk gave him. Hawk had been an easy target to lash out at.

The guys from the pool table tumbled out of the door and into the parking lot. They stopped laughing midstream as they laid their gazes his way.

"Hey, are you okay?" One guy came forward.

Phoenix put up a hand and forced his legs to remain stable under him. He didn't bother answering the young guy staring at him with wide eyes. Instead, he turned his back and focused on one foot in front of the other.

He had to go somewhere. Anywhere from here before he got himself in trouble he couldn't get out of.

PHOENIX STOPPED ON THE SIDEWALK. He wasn't sure how he got there. He hadn't been thinking about the direction his feet took him. He had kept walking until he found himself staring at Mack's house.

The beer buzz still fuzzed out his brain. He should turn right around and walk home or go up to the beach and sleep on a bench. He wouldn't be the first person to do that.

But his chest ached for her. When he was with her, the unsettled thoughts seemed to silence. She could tell him who he was without the fire department. He'd only ask that one question, then he'd go.

The bungalow's windows were dark. She was probably tucked in for the night. He wouldn't mind seeing her wrapped in a robe or a cute nightie thing. He wasn't entirely sure what she slept in. Their nights together kept them tangled in each other and the sheets. Clothes hadn't been a thought.

He knocked on the door. She didn't answer. He tried again but didn't want to ring the bell and wake the boys. He dug his phone out of his pocket and sent a text.

Are you awake? On your porch.

She didn't respond. He turned to go.

The creak of a door opening stopped him.

"Why are you here, Phoenix?"

"I needed to see you. Can I come in?"

He held his breath and waited for her answer.

CHAPTER SIXTEEN

*M*ack couldn't believe Phoenix was on her porch at this hour. Her stomach twisted with excitement and something else closer to worry. The porch light illuminated his glassy and hooded eyes. He swayed on his feet, and the sour smell of beer drifted to her.

"Are you drunk?" She checked over his shoulder for his truck, but the street was empty of it.

"I was drinking, but that was a while ago. I'm better now. Can I come in?" His words were slow but iced with the sadness of despair.

She should send him packing. She'd already said they couldn't be together. To have to say it again would tear her in two. There was nothing left for them now. She had her boys to worry about with the court date only days away. And what would it look like if one of them woke up and found Phoenix on the couch?

"Just keep it down. The boys are asleep." She stepped

back and held the door wider. Her heart was untrustworthy. It betrayed her in seconds.

With him in her home and hurting from something, she'd want to comfort him because she missed him. Those feelings could lead to him in her bed. Which could not happen.

"Thanks." He brushed past her. Her fingers fluttered near his shoulder, but her other hand yanked them away.

"Did you cut your face?" She turned on the table lamp. His cheek was red and spotted with scratches. Was it the hand of another woman that did that damage?

He wiped his cheek and shrugged. "Lost my balance."

"What happened?" She changed her mind. She didn't want to hear about it if it involved a woman.

"Nothing. I fell." He flopped down on the couch. "Come sit next to me."

She went into the kitchen and wet a paper towel. He had no reason to lie to her. He could barely stand on his feet. The effort to make up stories in his state would be too great. She could take his word that he had fallen. The pavement could have caused those marks.

"Here. Clean your face." She backed away before her fingers accidentally brushed his. She leaned against the wall and tugged her sweater closed.

He crumpled the paper in his hand but said nothing.

"Phoenix, why are you here?"

He stared at the ground then brought his gaze up to hers. Dark circles hung like burnt crescent cookies under his eyes. His cheek was bruised too. Her heart reached out to him, but her brain stopped it. Her warring body parts were wearing her out.

"Give us another chance." His words were barely a whisper.

"I can't. Not now." Each word cut her soul. It was a lie, but she didn't have another choice.

He pushed off the couch and stood before her. She forced her hands to stay put instead of running over his broad chest. She wanted to know what happened to him tonight, but he wasn't her responsibility. He would have to take care of himself.

"Tell me you don't have feelings for me, and I'll go." He pushed a piece of her hair off her face.

His touch sent delicious shivers over her skin. "I will always care about you."

"Look at me." His voice was low and hoarse.

She made her gaze lift to his.

"Say it. Tell me you don't feel what I feel when we're together."

"You've been drinking. Let's talk about this another time."

"I'm sober enough to know what I'm doing. I won't forget anything that happened tonight. I need to hear you say you don't want to be with me. That you don't feel the connection anymore."

"It doesn't matter. A relationship can't work now."

"It matters to me. Tell me. Tell me I didn't force you into anything."

Her words thrown back at her took her breath away. She had been scared in the parking lot of the police station. Her whole life had tilted and spilled when she was being booked for a crime. If it hadn't been for Phoenix and the mayor, she would have spent the night in jail and lost the boys for good. She owed him something for that.

"I shouldn't have said that to you. It was wrong. I went to bed with you of my own choice." It was more than just a choice. It had been a feeling she couldn't control. He was the ignitor to her flame.

Making love to him was also so much more than going to bed. She had cheapened what they had by saying something so cold and without emotion.

"So, you do feel the same way about me." He narrowed his eyes.

"I'm not saying that exactly. I'm saying..." She didn't know what she was saying. He stood too close to her. She couldn't think with him taking up all the air.

He didn't understand that her feelings couldn't count. Elliott and Ian were all that mattered. She would always pick them over him. Her life wasn't hers, and David threatened all she held dear.

"I love you." He cupped her face and whispered.

"Don't say that. It isn't true." She peeled his hands away. She tried to back up, but the wall stopped her.

Her words slashed pain across his face. He expected her to say something else, and she knew she couldn't. She had to make her point no matter what it cost her. "Go home, Phoenix."

The light in his eyes shut off. He turned away without another word.

The front door closed on a click.

She slid to the ground and rested her head on her knees.

She had brought this on herself. She had no one else to blame. Someday she'd be over this.

That day wasn't today.

CHAPTER SEVENTEEN

*M*ack pulled a tray of orange cranberry muffins from the oven and carried them out to the front of the bakery. The line at the cash register went to the door. If customers weren't staring at their phones, then they tapped their feet, shifting back and forth at the long wait. Everyone was in a hurry. Except, it seemed, her.

Today was the day. In one hour, she would be standing before the family court judge. A complete stranger held her fragile future in his hands. She wasn't ready to hear her fate. If there had been a way to postpone this moment forever, she would've done it. The information she had against David might not be enough, but it was all she had. She couldn't prove he was anything other than a caring father because that was how he wanted everyone to see him. He had been a master manipulator. By the time she had suspected something was wrong, she was knee deep.

Carlos pushed through the swinging doors from the

kitchen area and stood next to her. Flour dusted the red bandana he wore to keep the sweat out of his eyes. With the ovens going for hours, the kitchen was several degrees hotter than the front.

"You okay, Missus?" Carlos took the tray from her and deposited it into the case.

"Carlos, for the millionth time, I'm not a missus. Just call me Mack like everyone else. And yes, I'm fine. Thank you for asking."

"You let me know if you need anything. I work late today and help Maggie. You don't worry about a thing. I lock up." Carlos emphasized his offer with a nod.

"Thanks."

"Mr. Phoenix is going with you to the court? You should not go alone." Carlos poured himself a coffee and held a cup out to her. She shook her head.

"He's busy today." She had hurt Phoenix too badly for him to ever want to help her. She thought about calling him all week but stopped every time when she remembered the way he looked at her when he left her house.

She had broken his heart. He had given her a part of him no one else ever saw, and she had not honored that. She'd destroyed his trust and his friendship. And she missed him so much her chest hurt.

"He's a good man. A hero." Carlos added milk to his coffee.

"Yes, he is." She should've told Phoenix how much she admired him and how much he meant to her.

She went back to her small office and locked the door. She allowed the tears to come for one full minute, then she wiped her face and changed her clothes. She had to appear professional and respectable before the judge. If she was going to lose, she'd lose with dignity.

The drive to the courthouse was too short. She was tempted to drive around the block again, but Aria waited for her on the courthouse steps. Aria would be her support person if things went sideways. The boys were at school. Liv had driven them and was ready to pick them up if the day dragged on. Virginia assured her, if David did win, she would be able to spend another night with the boys before he could take them. Liv was under instructions not to hand over the boys to David no matter what he might say. Mack would be the one to place her children in his car. She would wring every last second out with them. Her stomach filled with acid just thinking about giving them away. She wanted to puke.

"It's going to work out," Aria said before Mack could get all the way to her.

"I can't take this. The private investigator was supposed to tell Virginia if he found out anything about David. If he didn't, then it's over. I've lost." She shivered inside her coat. The gray sky threatened to bring raw rain that dampened every surface.

"You're not going to lose. And if the worst does happen, you can appeal. You're not alone in this. Your family is here for you, including Hawk." Aria pulled her into a hug.

The person she really wanted with her if things got too difficult wasn't ever going to be there. Phoenix's confidence would have been the thing to lean against. He held her up when she was down. He had accepted the worst about her and still cared about her. He had never doubted her, but she had doubted herself, and that doubt was what broke them apart.

She and Aria climbed the rest of the steps to the glass doors. Every time she lifted her leg, it was as if she plowed through two feet of snow.

The front lobby was wide with a few offices stationed around it. The courtroom was to the right and large for such an old building as if it could've been a theater once. She hesitated outside the double wooden doors.

Aria turned with a reassuring smile and waved her in. She focused on Aria's assurance and forced herself forward into the room that smelled of wet socks and rotten wood. She conjured images of her bakery with its sugar and vanilla charm and filled with her customers. Her heart picked up speed with each step. This was it, and there was no going back. The breath left her. She grabbed Aria's hand.

The room was lined with rows of individual chairs made from wood and leather. Probably where the rotted smell came from. All the seat cushions were cracked and broken. The judges' bench ran the width of the front of the room. It allowed the judge to sit up higher than the people in the chairs. Two tables for lawyers and their clients were just beyond the broken seats. Virginia stood there in her immaculate black suit, pulling files from her briefcase. Her hair cascaded down her back. David's lawyer was at the other table, but no David.

"I'll be right here." Aria hugged her again. Aria's pregnant belly crowded the space between them.

The tears threatened again. It had only been a blink

ago when she had been pregnant with the twins. She couldn't miss seeing them tumble from their beds every morning. The nights would go on forever if she couldn't stop in their rooms to check on them. David didn't know how Ian liked his sandwiches cut or the order of Elliott's blankets on his bed.

"I can't do this." She stayed in the hug, afraid if she let go of her sister, she'd fall to the floor.

"You've got this," Aria said.

"Hey, I thought you could use some more moral support." The voice was so familiar her body stiffened.

But the voice didn't belong to Phoenix. Hawk stood beside her in his navy-blue suit. He placed a kiss on Aria's cheek, and she smiled into the eyes of her husband. They were perfect together. They had been through a terrible time, including the divorce, and found their way back to each other, but that was because Hawk wouldn't give up. He had fought for Aria.

Mack looked over her shoulder at the entryway into the courtroom. Phoenix's absence was his way of saying he'd given up on her. Because she'd forced him to.

"Thanks for coming." The words scraped her throat. She was glad Hawk had shown, but it wasn't enough to calm her frayed nerves.

"Mack, good. You're here." Virginia waved her over.

She took the seat beside her lawyer and wiped her hands on her thighs. "Did you hear back from the private investigator?"

Virginia grabbed her sweat-slicked hands. Virginia must be able to feel her sodden skin and want to pull away. She certainly did.

"Not yet. He said he'd be here. We still have a few minutes."

"Why isn't David here?"

Virginia checked over her shoulder. "I don't know. Let's focus on you. Remember, I'm going to explain to the judge about your relationship with the children and how separating you from them will be detrimental to them."

"Is that going to be enough?"

"We'll see."

A tall man in a gray suit hurried toward them. The top of his dress shirt was unbuttoned and absent of a tie. He parted his neat and brushed salt and pepper hair on the side. He carried a folder under his arm.

"Virginia, I've got what we need," the man said.

"Make my day, Bradley."

"I'm Bradley, your investigator." He held out his hand to Mack.

She shook it. His grip was firm and cold from the brisk weather outside.

He opened the folder and kept his voice low. "Okay, here goes. I did some checking. A baby boy was born in California to Todd and Carrie Hubert in nineteen seventy-five. Two years later the baby died in his sleep. Todd and Carrie divorced and never spoke to each other again. Todd died ten years ago of cancer. He had a hospice nurse by the name of Charles Finnigan whom he confided in about the baby he lost. Mr. Hubert had never gotten over the loss of his child or the loss of his marriage. He'd never remarried or had more children. He was alone at the time of his death except for the people paid to help him."

"Did you find something?" Aria leaned over the railing separating the visitor chairs from the defendant table.

"Aria, shush. Go sit down," Mack said.

"We want to hear too. You can't leave us out." Aria put an arm around Hawk.

"Oh, fine. Please, Bradley continue. My sister and her husband can hear whatever you're going to say."

He nodded at Aria and Hawk and continued. "Ten years ago, Charles Finnigan disappeared. I couldn't find a trace of him. However, David Hubert did resurface. A California driver's license was issued using the birth certificate belonging to David Hubert whose parents are Todd and Carrie. That license had a picture of a much younger David." He pulled out the photo of the license.

She took the paper and studied it. There was her ex-husband almost twenty years ago staring into the camera. It matched the picture on her phone.

She handed the paper back, not wanting to touch it any longer. "But that wasn't what David told me his parents' names were."

"Right." Bradley held up a finger. "I checked on the names on the gravestones you told Virginia about. Those people never resided in California. They also never had any sons. Three girls. Jessa, Elizabeth, and Shelby." He produced another document showing residences for the other set of Huberts listed on the gravestone.

"David Hubert got a Texas license shortly after the California one. From there another in New Jersey. It's probably in his wallet right now. Your ex-husband isn't who he says he is."

"What about his time in the Army?" Her voice shook with the anticipation of what this could mean for her and the boys.

"There has never been a David Hubert in the military. However, Charles Finnigan was honorably discharged in nineteen forty-five."

"Those dates don't add up," Aria said.

"The Charles Finnigan identity was most likely stolen as well. I can't prove he created documents, but he must've had something to convince an employer to hire him. For the right amount of money, it isn't difficult to get a new identity." He turned to Mack. "I am sorry to tell you I don't know who your ex-husband actually is, but he won't have any rights to your children."

She slumped in the chair. She had done it. She had actually found what she needed to save her family.

Her head reeled with conflicting emotions. Joy bubbled in her chest, but bile burned her throat too. David had made a fool of her. She had allowed a sociopath to touch her, to lie beside her, to have sex with her. Tears burned the back of her eyes.

Aria placed a hand on her shoulder. "Mack, are you okay?"

She might never be okay again.

"Sit tight," Virginia said. "Bradley and I need to get this information to the judge." The two hurried from the room using a door behind the bench. David's lawyer jumped up and ran after them.

"He lied to me. What am I going to tell the boys?" Her children would be devastated once they understood what

David had done. David had given no thought at all to how he might hurt his children. But he was ready to steal them from her without a thought. Her insides shook. He deserved to rot in jail for all she cared.

"You don't have to say anything yet," Aria said. "Take some time to process this."

"They're going to arrest him," Hawk said.

"Why isn't he here?" Aria looked around the room.

"He must realize his time is up. He had dropped the boys at school Monday morning, and I haven't heard from him since. Honestly, I hadn't given it a thought. I was so grateful not to have to deal with him this week. I didn't even miss him." She had never missed David. Not from the second she walked out of that house with the help of her sisters.

She did miss Phoenix with every fiber of her being. She wanted to call him and tell him her good news. He would not want to hear from her. Maybe one day they could go back to being friends. That might kill her, but she wouldn't be able to avoid him forever.

Virginia and Bradley returned. David's lawyer followed with his head hung. Virginia's smile rivaled the best sunrise.

"It's over. The judge didn't need to hear anymore. He's awarding full custody to you effectively immediately. They're going to put a warrant out for David's arrest. It's a crime to impersonate someone. Even if that person died over forty years ago. Congratulations." Virginia swooped her into a hug.

She still owed her lawyer so much. "I'll get you that money I owe you." Phoenix hadn't finished the repairs on the house, but she might still get a loan with the little he had done.

"I'll invoice you. You can make payments. But let's not worry about that now. Go celebrate with your family. And hug those boys for me."

She couldn't wait.

CHAPTER EIGHTEEN

*M*ack closed Ian's bedroom door and rested her head against it. Her body shook with relief. Her boys were in their rooms in her house sound asleep. Aria, Hawk, and Liv were in her kitchen, laughing amongst the dirty dishes, empty glasses, and half-eaten cake. Yet her heart still hurt.

She pushed away from the door and found her family. Hawk had an arm around Aria's shoulders. Liv sat at the table with her feet up on a chair. Her hair hung around her face. She downed the last of the beer. Their conversation swirled together with love and happiness like a well-made cake. Only her sister Blair was missing from this celebration. She would call her tomorrow and tell her the good news. Mack let out a long breath. Blair wasn't the only one missing. The room seemed empty without Phoenix's strong presence.

"Hey, are the boys asleep?" Aria moved away from Hawk's embrace. Her hand smoothed over her belly.

"Yeah. Thanks again for today. I don't think I could've done it without all of you."

"You did the hard part," Liv said. "Breaking and entering isn't easy to accomplish." She winked.

"I didn't break. Only entered." She forced a smile to her lips, then gathered some of the dishes needing something to do with her hands. She filled the sink with warm water and soap.

She hadn't entered David's house alone any more than she had sat in court alone today. If it hadn't been for Phoenix, she might not have gone through with her crazy idea to find what was in that heating duct. Today could've ended differently. She could be in this house by herself.

Aria grabbed some of the glasses and brought them to the sink. "Will you be okay if Hawk and I head home? My feet and back are killing me."

"Yes. Go. Go. I can take care of all of this." She waved her arm toward the kitchen table.

"Are you sure?" Aria said.

"Yes. Thank you." She pulled Aria into a hug but didn't linger. Her fragile emotions threatened to break into pieces.

Hawk leaned in and kissed her on the cheek. "Great job today."

She fought the urge to ask about Phoenix. She hoped he was okay after their last encounter. She couldn't bear the idea that she had hurt him so badly. At the time she thought she didn't have a choice. But now that she had won, maybe if she tried to explain again, he could forgive her.

Liv dropped her feet to the floor and pushed out of the

chair. "I'm going home with the lovebirds."

"You're not staying here?" The plan had been for Liv to stay with her while she was in town. Their time together was always cut short.

"They have an extra bed. You have a couch. And not that I don't love your munchkins to death, but a five a.m. wake-up call by two five-year-olds that smell like milk isn't exactly what I call a good morning. I'll be back tomorrow."

"I was hoping we could stay up all night and gossip like we used when we were kids. You can sleep in my room. I'll take the couch." If she were alone, the walls might swallow her up. Or she might break down and call Phoenix. With Liv around, she'd be less likely to cave to temptation.

"Okay, fine." Liv rolled her eyes, but her smile spread wide.

Liv exchanged hugs with Aria and Hawk. Mack's phone rang in the other room. "I've got to get that," she said over her shoulder.

The spicy taste of hope had her running into the kitchen, but the call was most likely Maggie or Carlos trying to find out how today went and if she'd be at work tomorrow. She had meant to call them when they returned, but in all the excitement it had slipped her mind.

Her phone vibrated against the counter. She reached for it and stopped.

David's name popped up on the screen.

~

PHOENIX STAYED IN THE SHADOWS. It wasn't too hard, since the streetlamp was up the road and what little light it offered did next to nothing to brighten the area around it. He had only hoped to catch a glimpse of Mack's smiling face. He was behaving like a crazy person hiding in the bushes, but he didn't want to interrupt her big moment by being seen. He wasn't welcomed anymore. She had made that clear the other night, but he couldn't seem to stop himself from walking over. His legs had taken him without any thought. Before he knew it, he was on Mack's street.

Mack, Hawk, and Aria had been back from court for hours. Hawk had texted him the news right after it had happened. Coming by her house now was not going to afford him the chance to see her, but he hoped maybe she'd walk her guests to the door when they left. Yeah, he was behaving like a child. It would be more mature to call and hang up when she answered.

Hawk and Aria came out of the house. They were speaking, but he couldn't hear what they were saying. Hawk held the car door for Aria then ran around the front of his truck. Phoenix longed for what they had. A family of his own. He had hoped it would include Mack and the boys, but that had been foolish. He should've stayed friends with her. Then he might be able to tell her how glad he was she'd won the case. Now he had to lurk like a sociopath.

Hawk's truck pulled away. It was time to go home too. He stole one more glance at the house, hoping to see Mack. She passed by the window. She was on the phone. Probably not giving him a second thought.

CHAPTER NINETEEN

"*D*avid, what do you want?" Mack forced her voice to stay calm. She hadn't bothered with the pleasantries. David was only calling because he wanted something.

"I know you think you won today."

"Why weren't you in court?" It shouldn't matter. He had no power over her any longer. She wanted someone to try and trace this call. Phoenix had friends in the police department. She needed him.

"I know what you found."

She ran through the living room past the front window, trying to find Liv. "You mean your fake ID?"

Liv was in the bedroom, staring at her phone. Mack snapped her fingers trying to get Liv's attention. Her head shot up. Mack mouthed David's name and pointed at the phone. Liv's mouth dropped open. Mack made a writing gesture in the air, hoping Liv would get some paper and a pen.

"You don't understand. I didn't have a choice."

"Where are you?"

Liv handed over a scrap of paper and a pen. She took it and jotted down to call Phoenix and tell him she needed help.

"I'm leaving again, but not before I give you what's coming to you."

She stood straight. "What?"

"You aren't going to get away with what you did. You had no right to take what wasn't yours. I gave you a good life, Mackenzie, and you tried to take mine. If you had just stayed married to me, we could be a family. You, me and the boys. But you had to listen to your sisters. They came between us. You would never have had the idea to snoop where you didn't belong before. You won't get away with ruining our lives."

Liv held up her phone and shook her head. No Phoenix. Where was he?

"What are you saying?"

"Pay attention. You will pay for what you did today and at my house. Just because your boyfriend got you out of trouble doesn't mean there isn't more coming. Be ready." He ended the call.

"What happened?" Liv said.

"I think he's out of his mind. He's mad that he lost." She looked at the phone to make sure the call was really over. Or better yet, had actually occurred.

"What did he say?" Liv's voice echoed throughout the bedroom.

"He said something about me paying for what I did to him, but he can't actually do anything. The police are looking for him. Right? Tell me it was just an idle threat."

She had gone too far this time in David's eyes. He had retaliated for far less in the past.

"It wouldn't hurt if you had a gun about now." Liv looked around as if a gun would materialize on the bed.

"Liv, seriously?"

"Sorry." She shook her head and waved her hands as if she could erase the nonsense running around in her head. "We're overreacting. What's he going to do? He can't be so stupid that he'd come here, could he?"

"No. No. That's ridiculous. He's just angry and wants to scare me. Which he did a pretty good job of." He was always good at scaring her. Telling her she wasn't good enough without him. Telling her no one would love her ever again. Trying to keep her from her family and friends.

She had been such a fool. She had completely lost herself during the time with David, and now it all made sense. He wasn't who he said he was; how could he possibly encourage her to be her true self?

"I should've been smarter, Liv. I let him manipulate me. What has he done to the boys?" Was the damage to her children irreversible? Or could they somehow come out of this untouched? What would she do when they started asking about their father and she couldn't give them a real answer? No child should live with the knowledge his father was a monster.

"Hey, that part of your life is over. It has been for a year or more now. He's gone for good. He didn't come to court. He won't come around here. He's just blustering. You know what? Call your lawyer and tell her David phoned and what he said. Maybe she can have a police car drive by a few times just to be safe."

"Good idea." She left a message on Virginia's voice-mail. "Should I call the police myself?"

"Can't hurt." Liv checked the window locks.

Mack called the non-emergency number and spoke to the sergeant on call. She explained what had happened, but his response sat somewhere between disinterested and bored. Idle threats in a sleepy shore town weren't high on the list of concerns.

"My brother-in-law is Hawk Egan, if that helps," she said. It couldn't hurt to throw his name around. Most of the police officers and firefighters knew each other. Maybe the guy would help the relative of a fellow first responder.

"I know Hawk. Phoenix's younger brother. I went to high school with Phoenix. Good guy. Do you know him?"

"We've met." She wanted to say *of course, dumb shit,* but that might not be the way to go.

"I'll let the detective on duty know. Say hello to the guys for me." The sergeant hung up.

"I might have to move out of town to get away from Phoenix. He's going to be around every corner." She tossed the phone on the bed and dropped down beside it.

The day had been a roller coaster of emotions with its ups and downs. Her life needed to take a turn toward the normal again. How would that ever happen? If the police didn't arrest David, she could be looking over her shoulder her whole life. Moving might have to be an option. It would be easier. Phoenix around every corner would be too much to bear.

"Let's have a glass of wine and forget all about it." Liv untangled Mack's fingers from her own hair and led her out of the bedroom.

"Phoenix didn't answer his phone?" She was a masochist when it came to him. It had been impulsive to call him. Heat burned her cheeks now. What could she possibly say to him or have him do that could protect her from David? She had overreacted. Probably exactly what David had wanted.

"I'm sorry. He might not have recognized the number." Liv poured the wine into two glasses.

"Did you send a text too?" She braced herself for the answer.

"I'm sorry, Mack. I did. He didn't respond." Liv glanced over the rim of her wine glass.

"I guess I deserve that. Next time I'll call Hawk."

"Yeah, that might be a good idea."

MACK COULDN'T BREATHE. Her chest hurt with each inhale. She had lain on the couch to get some sleep after cleaning up the party in the kitchen only minutes ago. Maybe it had been longer, but she wanted to keep sleeping. She blinked her eyes open. The laundry room off the kitchen glowed orange. Cracking and snapping woke her up the rest of the way, but her mind couldn't register what was happening. She tried to get some air in her lungs and gagged. The room smelled like smoke. *Smoke.* She fell off the couch and covered her mouth with the collar of her shirt. The house was on fire. *Holy fuck. Move.* She commanded her brain.

She had to get to the kids and to Liv. Panic tangled her legs under her, but the need to survive propelled her forward. She ran down the hall and threw open the door to her room. "Liv, get up. Get up." She grabbed Liv's arm and tugged.

"What are you doing?"

"The house is on fire."

"What?" Liv jumped from the bed. "I need shoes."

"Hurry. I have to get the boys. Do you have your phone? Call 9-1-1. Hurry." She had left her phone on the table by the couch. She needed to get the boys first. Then she could grab her phone to call for help if needed.

She ran from the room and threw her shoulder into Ian's door. The door banged against the wall, and she lost her balance before righting herself. The bed was a dark square in the corner of the room lit by a small night light.

She shook him. "Ian, wake up."

"I'm sleeping, Mommy." He rubbed his eyes.

"Come on, buddy. We have to get out of the house now." She hoisted him to his feet. There wasn't even time to get their coats. She grabbed the blanket and threw it over his shoulders. "Let's go."

"Is something bad happening?" Her intuitive little boy couldn't be fooled.

"It's not good. Just stay by me."

Together they went into Elliott's room. "Elliott, get up." She didn't wait for Elliott to respond. She slid her arms under him and heaved his solid body against her chest.

"Mommy, where are we going?" Elliott's voice croaked with sleep.

"Outside." She grabbed his blanket too.

"I need Mr. Thomas." Elliott lunged for the stuffed elephant, almost falling out of her arms. She struggled to hold him and placed him on his feet before he clocked his head on the floor.

"I need a toy too." Ian turned to run for his room.

"We don't have time." She gripped the collar of his pajamas and tugged him back. His feet left the ground, and he collided with her legs. They were going to burn to death. She didn't have time for better parenting skills and explanations.

"Take one of my toys." Elliott handed over his stuffed giraffe. Ian clutched it to his chest.

"Thank you, Elliott." Ian patted Elliott's head.

Tears threatened to come. Her precious angels needed to be safe.

She ushered them toward the living room, away from the flames that had grown since she left it. The crackling of the fire pursued them like a demon. The smoke was thick and made it harder to breathe.

"Get down." She yanked the boys to the floor where the air was thinner. "Hold onto me. Don't let go no matter what, okay, boys?" The room was dark and filled with smoke. It was getting harder to see even with the flames spreading light behind them.

"Why is the house on fire?" Ian said.

"Are we going to catch on fire?" Elliott's little voice shook.

"Just hold on to Mommy and keep moving. We're

going to be fine." She prayed she didn't just lie to her children. Had Liv called for help?

Two little hands grabbed her clothes. She kept going.

"Liv? Where are you?" Her words came out in coughing spurts.

"At the front door."

She didn't like the sound of Liv's voice. "What's wrong?" She kept moving forward until she bumped into the couch.

She had to backtrack and go around it without losing the boys. Her phone was still on the table. She smacked the air with her palm until it landed on the wood with a crack. Where was it? She needed to call. Her fingers slid across the glass of the screen. She pulled the phone against her chest. Relief washed over her as the picture of the boys popped up. With trembling hands, she found her list of favorites and hit the call button.

"The door won't open." Terror coated Liv's voice in thick strokes.

"What do you mean? Of course, it will." She dropped the phone and went to Liv.

She helped the boys to sit against the wall. "Don't move, either one of you."

She turned the knob, but the door wouldn't budge. "What the hell?" She pulled and twisted and pulled again. It was stuck. Panic reached down her throat and grabbed her heart.

"Why won't it open, Mack?"

"I don't know." It didn't make sense.

The only other door was off the kitchen and going that way would be dangerous. "The window," she said.

They could go out her bedroom window. She ushered the boys in front of her. "Liv, hold onto my shirt." She pushed the boys toward the bedrooms again.

The smoke continued to thicken and make it harder to breathe. They all coughed out the dirty air, but they didn't have time to crawl. Inside the bedroom, she shut the door, hoping for a few extra seconds.

Liv threw open the window. The cold, clean salt air rushed in. Relief crashed over her like the ocean waves.

"I'll climb out first. You hand the boys to me," Liv said.

The drop from the window was short. It was a good plan. Liv put one leg out then the other and jumped. Mack held her breath.

"Okay, send out the boys."

Mack stuck her head out the window. Liv was waiting with her hands up. They would freeze out there in their pajamas and socked feet. But they could run down the street to her neighbor for help.

"Here we go." She lifted Ian around the waist. "Put your leg over the window. Aunt Livvie will catch you."

Ian nodded and did as he was told. Her faithful rule follower made her heart squeeze. He was far too serious for such a little boy. With Ian safely on the ground, she hoisted Elliott next. "Ready?"

Elliott threw his elephant first. "Catch Mr. Thomas, Aunt Livvie. He's afraid of the fire."

Liv caught the toy and gave it to Ian. "Come on, little man. I'll catch you."

Elliott leaned out the window headfirst. Mack tried to help him get his legs around, but he dove out instead. She bit back a scream and lunged toward the window too.

Liv was on her back with her arms around Elliott.

"Are you okay?" She gulped in the cold air.

"Yes. Please get out of there," Liv said.

She took a final glance at the room. Her whole life was here. Every memory of her life after David. Her pictures. Her jewelry. Her laptop with her clients' information. Pictures of cakes she had decorated. Her breath caught.

She stuck her head out the window. "Call for help and go to the street. I'll be right out. I have to get Pop's recipes."

She didn't wait for Liv, but Liv's voice screaming her name followed her back into the fire.

CHAPTER TWENTY

The phone rang somewhere in the distance. Phoenix hoped it would stop. He wanted to stay asleep. But the ringing continued, not allowing him another second of peace. The clock on the table with its red numbers said a call at this hour couldn't be good. He reached for the phone as the ringing stopped. The missed call name gave him pause. Mack had hung up.

He started to unlock the screen and call her back but stopped. If her call had been important, she would've stayed on the line or left a message. She could've accidentally hit his name from the contact list or from an older call and hadn't meant to reach out at all. He flopped back on the bed. If it was important, she'd call back.

The phone rang again. A smile crept across his face. Maybe she missed him and couldn't sleep either. She wanted to tell him before another minute passed. He hit the answer button without paying attention to the screen.

"Hey." He tried to play it cool.

"I need you." Hawk's deep voice startled him.

"What's the matter?" His brother was the last person he expected to call. He sat up again.

"There's a fire."

"Shit. Is that why you're calling? I can't, man. You know that." Was his brother trying to torture him? Using tough love as a way for him to deal with his issues? Fuck that. He was through. He would never wear his gear again.

"Phoenix, shut up and listen. It's Mack's house. The call just came in. We're hopping on the truck now. You need to get there."

"Mack's house? Are you sure?" He shoved his legs into his jeans. His knee didn't even feel the pressure.

"Never more. See you in five." Hawk ended the call.

Mack needed him. That was why she had called. Dread ran its cold hand down his back. If she hadn't waited for him to answer, she must be in trouble. He ran out of the house without a coat and jumped into his truck. His house was closer to hers than the firehouse was. He hit the gas pedal and floored it. Hopefully, he wasn't too late.

MACK YANKED open the bedroom door. The hallway was black and dark. The smoke had filled the area like a fleece blanket. She couldn't see her hand in front of her face. The fire raged with angry cracks and snaps, making it hard to think.

The recipes were in the kitchen cabinet at the opposite end of the laundry room. It was stupid, but she had to have them. Her grandfather's recipes were all she had of him. His love for baking had helped her be the person she was today.

She turned into the living room and banged into a door. Her head spun. This wasn't the living room. She groped the space before her. Her heart climbed into her throat, choking the air from her. Or rather the smoke. She smacked into the sink with one hand. Her other hand gripped something plastic. The shower curtain. She had walked into the bathroom instead.

The whole idea to get to the kitchen was crazy. She needed to get out of the house. Her heart broke for the lost recipes, but she couldn't die now. Not after she had won her case and had her boys forever. If she died, she would miss out on every moment of their lives. She had to be there to help them grow up and become men. Strong men. Honest men. Men who knew how to love. Men like Phoenix. If she made it out of this alive, she would tell Phoenix what a fool she had been for ever letting him go.

Panic and fear pushed her out of the bathroom. The smoke was thicker in the hallway than when she had gone in, if that was even possible. She struggled to breathe and continued to cough. The blackness swallowed her up. Was the bedroom to the left or the right? It should be to her right. She kept her back to the wall and inched along it hoping to find another bedroom. She could climb out any window in one of those rooms. Except the wall ended, and she was in the living room, staring at the flames.

CHAPTER TWENTY-ONE

*P*hoenix jumped out of his truck and ran toward Mack's house. The flames were coming out of the roof in the back corner. The laundry room was on fire. The spot closest to the fire would be several hundred degrees and building smoke at a rapid rate.

Liv and the boys ran toward him. His legs almost gave out with relief.

"Phoenix, thank God you came. You have to get Mack." Liv threw herself into him.

He grabbed her arms to keep her from bouncing backward and landing on her ass. "What are you talking about? Where's Mack?"

"She went back in for Pop's recipes. I tried to stop her, but she took off. She hasn't come out." Liv's chest heaved with each word.

The ladder truck sped down the street, breaking the night's silence with sirens and horns. The lights spun their brightness over trees and rooftops with each flash.

Neighbors in their pajamas and clutching robes to their chests in the cold gathered on the sidewalk.

He wanted his gear. The thought stopped him for a second. He glanced back at the house. Mack needed him. His fears would have to shut the hell up. He wasn't going to let her die. Not on his watch. Ever.

Hawk jumped off the truck first. Phoenix didn't wait but ran to his brother. "Give me my stuff. Mack's inside."

He shoved his legs and arms into his fire coat and pants. He heaved the heavy oxygen tank onto his back and snapped the belt around his waist.

"Are you sure?" Hawk grabbed his arm.

"Hurry with the water. Break open the back to let the flames loose. It's coming from her laundry room. The wind could shift off the ocean and send the smoke and flames in the opposite direction too quickly. I'm going in the front door. I might have a chance that way. I've got to get her."

"You need the handline." Hawk called after him.

"No time."

"You're going to get disoriented within ten feet."

"I'll be fine." He had to trust himself.

For Mack.

PHOENIX HAD ten minutes at best. Without knowing the source of the fire, he couldn't tell how fast it would move. But everything in its path was an accelerant. The heat and flames could be compromising the roof and the floors. Mack could have fallen into her crawl space. Or the attic could collapse on both of them. His heart picked up speed, and his breath came in short gasps. He needed to slow down, or he'd use up all his oxygen too quickly. There was no time to panic.

He checked the front door for heat and wanted to be sick. A bungee cord had been tied around the door handle and nailed into the side of the house. *What the fuck?*

He kicked the door in and promised himself to deal with it later. The flames toward the back of the house were orange and red. They mixed behind the screen of black smoke. The smoke was thick and made seeing past the living room difficult. The area was stifling with heat. Wherever Mack was, she wouldn't last much longer. He hoped she had at least found the bathroom and soaked herself with water.

"Mack?" He pictured the layout of the rooms with their windows and doors. As long as she wasn't in the area where the fire was, they had a chance.

He tripped over the corner of the couch in his hurry to find her. The pain shot up his knee and into his groin. His eyes squeezed shut while he waited for the pain to pass.

He righted himself and took a deep breath. She used the room off to the left as an office. It was supposed to be a dining room so it was long. The hallway to the bedrooms was behind that. Three bedrooms and two bathrooms. The place wasn't big. She didn't have a lot of places to go. She could even be outside by now. He needed to keep moving forward to find out.

He kept the handle of his flat head axe in front of his face to keep from banging into a wall. "Mack?" He tried again.

Where the hell was she? The smoke in the office was thinner and made seeing a little easier. The room was empty except for the furniture and her belongings. He went back into the thick smoke.

"Mack? Are you in here?" He was wasting air by calling out to her. If she was conscious, she might not hear him over the flames and through his mask.

He took a chance and went in the direction he believed the kitchen was. The smoke was too thick to see through the flames, but the increase in crackling and splitting gave him an indication he was going the right way.

Sweat broke out over all of his body as he approached. She wouldn't be alive if she had gone this way. The heat would stifle her lungs. The darkness would throw her off. She wouldn't be able to find her way back, but he had to know. He wouldn't leave her here no matter what.

He got as close as he could. "Mack? Mack, please answer me." He begged. He would beg her to take him back when he found her. He would find her. Alive. He had to.

Out of habit, he reached for a handline, but his hand met the air. Where was he? He needed help. He couldn't get lost in here. Not like before.

The hallway to the bedrooms would be the saving grace. From the kitchen it was to the right. Around a corner. Or he could end up in the office again. Or back where he started. His oxygen tank beeped a warning.

"Mack?" He yelled until his throat hurt.

This could all be for nothing. If his team were here, someone could tell him if she found his way out. Where were they? They were taking too long to get inside. Or maybe he wasn't in the house as long as he thought. He hadn't checked the oxygen level in the tank before he put it on. He might not even have the full ten minutes he thought he had.

He hurried in the direction he hoped the hallway was.

The tank continued to beep.

His heart hammered around in his chest, wanting out as much as he did. Sweat ran down his neck and back. He wasn't leaving this structure until he found her or was convinced she had made it to safety. If he died trying, so be it. All that mattered was Mack. Her boys needed her.

He swung the axe handle and hit air to his left. Could be a bedroom. He turned.

And tripped over something on the floor.

Like before.

CHAPTER TWENTY-TWO

*M*ack gave up. She couldn't find her way out. Every turn brought her nowhere. It hurt to breathe. Her eyes stung. Her lungs ached for clean air. She had been crawling around on the floor for what seemed like an eternity.

She had prayed to find the bathroom where she could fill the tub with water, but she only managed to end up in Ian's room over and over. At least she thought it was Ian's room. Tears burned her eyes. She would never see her children again.

She tried to scream, but the sound dried up before it left her mouth. She curled up on her side and closed her eyes. The carbon monoxide would make her fall asleep. She'd die from suffocation before the flames got her. She was too tired to keep going.

Maybe the fire department was on its way. Maybe Phoenix would save her. She wished she could see him one more time too.

Something moved.

She tried to sit up, but her head was too heavy to lift.

Her side split with pain. Something large and heavy had collided into her. A whoosh and thud landed beside her.

Someone breathed heavy. She reached out and grabbed a leg.

"Holy shit," the person said. A man. "Mack?"

"Phoenix?" Her voice croaked. Had he come or was she hallucinating? Is that what happened when the air was impossible to breathe?

"Don't talk. I'm here. I'll help you. I have oxygen."

He put something to her nose and mouth. A sweet smell hit her nose first. She drank in the fresh air. Her hands reached out to him. Her fingers met his mask. She couldn't see his eyes very well, but he seemed to be crying too.

"Don't take that off, no matter what. I don't have a lot of oxygen left in the tank. It wasn't full when I got here. So we have to hurry. I'm going to find the way out. We need a window. Just nod. Do you know where we are?"

She did as he asked.

"Okay, A bedroom I hope?"

She nodded again and continued to suck down the oxygen. She wouldn't let her gaze leave his face behind that mask.

"I'm going to carry you." He started to stand.

She grabbed his strong arm and tried not to break down. He'd come for her. He had saved her. She had so much she needed to say to him and now might be her only chance.

A loud crack that shook the house vibrated up her spine.

"We're out of time," Phoenix said.

EITHER THE ROOF had caved in or Hawk and the guys had finally gotten inside. Either way, it didn't matter. They couldn't go and check. He and Mack needed a window and now. He scooped her up in his arms and didn't give one shit if she wanted to walk on her own. He would carry anyone in her situation, but her most of all, the woman he loved.

He used his better leg and kicked until he hit a wall. The first bedroom had windows on the back wall. He just needed to find that wall.

"Mack, run your hand over the wall as I move. Tell me when you find the window."

They moved along. Each step the oxygen tank reminded him they were on borrowed time. Two people using from the same tank would only finish it off faster.

He tried to take another step, but she signaled him. If he was a praying man, he'd be thanking a benevolent god.

"I have to put you down and get the window open." He placed her beside him so he could move without disconnecting the oxygen.

The window glided up in his touch. Fresh air rushed in. Relief buckled his knees.

"You're going to have to let go of the oxygen. I'll give you a boost up, and you climb out the window. Got it?"

She nodded.

He helped her over the windowsill.

His radio hissed with static. "Phoenix, are you in there?" Hawk's voice echoed in his helmet.

"On my way out."

"Your tank is almost out," Hawk said.

"I'm fine. Climbing out the back window now." He hoisted himself into the open window and nose-dived onto the grass.

He pushed off the ground. His knee complained about the landing. Mack threw herself into his arms and knocked him back to the ground.

He held her close.

He wasn't ever going to let her go again.

CHAPTER TWENTY-THREE

*M*ack sat in the back of the ambulance. Men in turn-out gear ran around her ruined house. Smoke still spiraled into the sky, but the fire was out. Her grandfather's recipes were no more. His box style lettering all written in pencil would be nothing but ash now. She wasn't even allowed to go near it and check. Her heart ached for the loss of the one thing she had left of the only real father figure in her life. All she had were the memories of him teaching her to bake. She would have to make an extra effort to teach the boys so Pop's legacy could live on. She would write down all the recipes she made daily at the bakery. Pop's recipes. Even though his handwriting was gone, his talent could live on.

The wind came in off the ocean and sent a deep chill over her skin and into her bones. Nothing could warm her up, but she wasn't ready to leave without Phoenix. If that meant sitting there inhaling oxygen the paramedics insisted she use even though she didn't think she needed it, so would inhale. Her life had turned to rubble in a few short hours. Someone had set that fire and she suspected she knew who.

The fire department put out the fire shortly after they had arrived. But the damage had been done. Between the smoke and the water, she and the boys would have to find another place to live.

Liv had taken the boys to Aria's about an hour ago. Mack had refused to go the hospital, so the ambulance hung around for her as a favor to Phoenix.

He walked up to her with his fire coat open and swinging behind him. His fire pants were tucked into his boots. His hair was stuck to his head from all the sweat. His high-voltage smile lit up his soot-covered face. He had never been so handsome.

"How are you feeling?" He brushed some of the hair off her face. His touch sent warm shivers over her skin that combatted the cold ocean air.

"I'm okay. Thanks to you." She had thought she was going to die, and as if she were in some movie, he had fallen right over her.

He sat beside her and gripped her knee. "I have some bad news. Do you want me to tell you now or later when you feel more up to it?"

"Tell me now, Phoenix. I don't want us to keep anything from each other ever again." She laced her fingers through his.

"What does that mean?" He narrowed his eyes.

"I know about the panic attacks. Hawk told me the night you two fought at the bar. He thought I should know. Why didn't you say something?" She had been too much of coward to call and check on him after that conversation. But after tonight, she would not wait to ask for what she wanted or speak her heart's truth ever again.

He let out a long breath and stared at the starless sky. "I thought I had it under control. I didn't want you to think I was anything less than a man."

She turned to face him and placed a hand on his scruffy cheek. "You are all man. You are strong, honest, kind. You put your life on the line for other people and ask nothing in return. You have done that with me over and over. You have been by my side through all my craziness with David and never once did you ask for anything for yourself. I'm sorry I didn't take better care of you. I'm sorry I wasn't there for you to share something so important as your fears. Please forgive me."

He squeezed her hand. "You don't have anything to be sorry for. I rushed you when you weren't ready. I should've been more sensitive to what you were going through. I promise to give you the space you need."

Hawk trotted up to them. "Hey. We're cleaned up and ready to head back to the station. Chief wants you to come too and help with the report. Mack, I'm sorry about the house, but you'll have a strong case for arson. I can get someone to give you a ride to my place."

"You're sure it's arson?" she said. "Isn't arson hard to prove?" She looked between the two brothers.

"You didn't tell her yet?" Hawk said.

"I was getting to that. I'll bring her to your house and then come over to the station. I'll see you in about a half hour." Phoenix stuck out his hand to his brother.

Hawk yanked him into a hug and slapped his back. "I'm glad you're okay. Thanks, Mack. If it hadn't been you,

I'm not sure he would've gone back in." Hawk kissed her on the cheek and hurried over to the fire truck.

The other guys waved, and the truck pulled away. The paramedics returned and took their oxygen back. They too drove away and left her and Phoenix standing on the street alone.

"Let me get you to Aria's. It's cold out here. I have a sweatshirt in the truck, if you want."

She slid her arms into his shirt and let the warm fleece swallow her up. His clean scent drifted out of the fabric. She brought the collar up to her nose and inhaled. His smell was all the oxygen she needed.

"You didn't finish telling me the bad news." She slid into the truck beside him. He blasted the heat and turned the vents toward her.

"I spoke with the chief. The fire started in the laundry room. Accelerant was used outside and inside. It looks like it was poured over a basket of clothes in there, as well. Mack, I'm sorry to have to tell you this, but your front door was rigged closed. Whoever started the fire wanted to trap you and the boys inside."

Her stomach turned sour. "How did he get in the house?"

"I don't know. Maybe while you were at court? You didn't hear anyone outside the door?" Phoenix turned off her street and weaved his way through town.

She hadn't. After Aria and Hawk left, she and Liv had sat on her bed with the television on and talked and talked. It had been hours before she finally collapsed on the couch. "He watched us. Are the police looking for him?"

"I told my chief what you said about the phone call. Tomorrow after the fire marshal comes and officially calls the fire arson, the police will be brought in to investigate. You'll have to tell your story again. It's going to be hard to prove it was David. He could very likely get away with it."

"And steal another identity? I can't let him do that to someone else."

"The police are looking for him on that charge. We might catch a break. In the meantime, I don't want you and the boys alone. Move in with me until David is caught."

"We can't do that. The boys take up too much space. You'd never get a minute's peace with all of us there. I'll find a place to rent." She hadn't thought beyond tonight but would have to start to.

She couldn't stay with Aria and Hawk. Their baby was coming soon. They needed to be a family without the addition of three more people. Liv would go back to her apartment in the city. It could be time for her to move on too. She couldn't risk David finding her. And Phoenix had said earlier he was giving her the space she needed, but she hoped that had changed.

He pulled up in front of Aria's house. The front light was on, but the house looked tucked in. She hated to wake them with a knock on the door. She couldn't even text now that she didn't have a phone.

"I promised myself, if I found you in that house and we got out alive, I would convince you to stay with me. So, please, don't say a word until I'm finished." He turned in his seat to face her.

"I love you, Mackenzie Scirocco. I have probably loved

you my whole life, but I didn't know it until recently. I realize I'm a little banged up these days. I'm not entirely sure I'll go back to work at the fire department, but I'm going to think about it. I hope you'll help me with that because when I'm with you, I'm calm and at peace. So, you're wrong when you say I wouldn't want you and the boys around. That's all I want. Us. Together. The four of us. I can try and be a good dad, if you want me to, and I hope you do."

"Phoenix, I—"

"Hang on. I'm not done. I want to protect you. Don't hate me for that. I can't help it. I'll feel better if you're with me until this thing with David is officially over. Then I hope you'll be so in love with me, you won't want to leave." He flashed his smile, and her heart melted.

"Can I talk now?"

"Sure."

"I should've said this a long time ago. I pushed you away because I was afraid I'd lose the boys, but while I was going through my own personal hell, it was you I wanted beside me. I didn't know how to make you see I'd made a mistake by pushing you away. You were so mad at me, but I was willing to let you go so you could be happy. I don't want to live without you. I don't know if I know how to even begin if you're not in my life, and I have a lot of starting over to do."

"Does that mean I can drive you back to my house right now and hold you all night?"

She glanced at the house then back at him. "Can you text Hawk and let him know so no one will worry?"

"Consider it done." He pulled his phone from the console and typed.

"There's nowhere else I want to be than with you, Phoenix."

"For now?"

"Forever. I love you."

∾

Dear Reader,

Thank you for reading Through the Darkness. I hope you enjoyed it as much as I enjoyed writing Mack and Phoenix's story. Please consider leaving an honest review. Reviews help authors.

Please turn the page for a sneak peek at the next book in the series—Light Upon the Darkness.

LIGHT UPON THE DARKNESS - CHAPTER ONE

Chapter One

He wanted to stand in the ocean because the salt-water waves were the only thing left to soothe his soul. Hudson Lozado parked his sedan in a diagonal spot in front of the boardwalk in Water Course and turned off the engine. The sun hadn't crested the horizon yet, leaving the sky in muted blacks and dark grays. He was always an early riser and couldn't stay another second in the stuffy apartment he had rented. So, he hopped on the Garden State Parkway over an hour ago to come home.

He had worked his ass off most of his life, and all he had to show for it were the suitcases in the trunk and the surfboard on the roof. The surfboard was a new edition. He hadn't surfed in fifteen years. Surfing was part of his life before. Before he lost it all the first time.

A first time existed because he lost it all again recently.

He pushed out of the car into the cold January morning. The wind whipped in from the water and coated him and the car with a light spray from the ocean. He grabbed his coat from the back and stepped onto the boardwalk. The old weather-worn boards creaked under his feet. The ocean rumbled its good morning with rough waves crashing against the sand. He forgot to buy a wetsuit. No winter ocean for him until he did.

As the sun climbed over the horizon, bringing with it the glow of golds and oranges the black sky began to fade away to make room for the new day. A few surfers in their full suits carried boards to the water and entered the ocean near the jetties. He was never a great surfer even though he had grown up at the beach.

His recent heart attack inspired him to revisit his old past-time. Life was too short he had learned at only thirty-six. He wanted to do only things he enjoyed, which meant quitting his job. He had donated all his suits too. He never wanted to wear a tie again.

He might've kept his job if his boss hadn't pissed him off. He had quit before he knew what he was saying. Now he had no job, no home, and a divorce under his belt. He was swinging for the fences.

The surfers waited patiently on their boards for the best wave to bring them in. Great surfers possessed the right amount of patience. He turned away with a small amount of regret and returned to his car. For the next several weeks, he planned on staying in his childhood house, spend as much time outside as possible, and relearn how to surf. After that, he wasn't sure. The idea that he had no plan for his future ignited a wild streak in him and made his palms sweat at the same time.

He navigated the narrow streets of town on his way to

Cedar Street and stopped in front of his family's old Victorian. "What the hell?"

A blue and white realtor sign littered the front lawn. The words *under contract* at the top had him wondering if he was seeing straight.

He pulled into the driveway and hopped out of the car. He approached the sign as if it might bite him. He rocked the sign with his finger. It creaked on its hinges. His father hadn't said one stinking word about selling the house.

He dug his phone out of his pocket and pulled up his father's number. The phone rang and rang. Just as he expected the voicemail to answer, his father picked up.

"Hello?" The voice he would recognize anywhere barked over the line.

"You didn't tell me the house was for sale." He didn't see the point in easing into the conversation. His father had some questions to answer.

"Hudson? Is that you?"

"Yes, Dad. It's me." He let out a long breath. "Why didn't you mention you were selling our home?"

"Why would I say anything to you? It's my house."

He scratched at the beard he had grown in since the heart attack. Before then, his job always required he keep a clean shave. "I tried to understand when you wouldn't fly up from Florida to see me in the hospital, but why wouldn't you tell me you decided to sell our home?"

"It's just a house, and you haven't lived there in some time. How did you know about the sale anyway?"

"I'm standing on the front lawn."

"Why are you there?"

"Because I wanted to come home." He wouldn't bother to go into how his recent reality check had him worried about his mortality, or how he really had nowhere else to go. And worse, he would never mention that when he was home, he felt closer to *her*.

"I'm closing in a week, but you can stay there if you want. The place is basically empty except for the junk in the attic. I have a garbage company coming to take everything up there away."

"Everything? Even Mom's stuff?" After his mother had died, his father had shoved most of his mother's belongings into the attic. She had barely been in the ground before all signs of her had been erased.

"You were always too sensitive. Just like her."

He ignored his father's dig. He had spent his entire life trying to be the kind of man his father had expected him to be, but often failed. If his father could see his beard and the length of his hair, he would cluck his tongue in disapproval. Wait until he found out that his only son quit his job and had purchased a surfboard.

"I want to go through whatever is up there." He had to make sure his father wasn't accidentally throwing away something valuable since he hadn't bothered to mark anything in the boxes when he packed Mom up.

If he were ever to have a child again, he would want his son or daughter to possess some of his mother's things. She had been so excited at the prospect of becoming a grandparent, and just as devastated as he was when things didn't work out.

"Why would you want to waste your time by going

through old boxes?" His father's gravel-filled voice brought him back to the front lawn.

"Because Mom deserves to be more than yesterday's trash."

"The items in the boxes are all garbage, but suit yourself. I'll be up at the end of the week for the closing. Good bye, Hudson."

"See ya." He ended the call.

He had one week to make his way through the attic and collect old memories. Where would he go after that? He had no place to live, but he wouldn't leave until he had opened every box in the attic. The new owners would just have to deal with him even if it meant dragging every box outside onto the lawn and looking through them there.

He hadn't asked his father, the man with ice water in his veins, why he picked now to sell the house. He stared at the house and then the surfboard as if they would have an answer for him. There didn't have to be a good reason for his father's decision. He had decided to sell and that was that. Dr. Lozado's son didn't factor into any part of it.

He grabbed his bags from the trunk. He might as well get started. He let himself in through the back. The back door opened to a staircase that led to the upstairs apartment. His father had designed it as a way for the family to come and go without having to go through the office and interact with patients.

This old house wouldn't be in his family anymore. He had grown up here. He had brought only one woman to this home to meet his parents. That woman would be glad to see this house become something other than the space for his father's medical practice. He wished he could tell her about the sale. Maybe if the right person in town found out, she or he would tell her.

While he had lain in that hospital bed after the heart attack, he had missed her—Liv—so much he had dialed her number several times but never hit the send button. She would not come to him. She had made that clear when she had left and chose a life without him. That moment had been so long ago, and yet it burned his soul like it was yesterday. He would never get over her.

The stairs groaned under his weight, no happier to greet him than his father was. The inside of the house was almost as cold as it was outside. He flipped on the light in the kitchen.

He dropped his bags on the floor. The thud echoed in the empty space. He wandered from room to room. His father hadn't exaggerated. Nothing was here except a single roll of toilet paper in the hallway bathroom.

"How the hell am I going to stay in this place?" He scratched at his beard again.

He searched all the closets and found a set of sheets and a blanket shoved to the back of a high shelf. He adjusted the thermostat for more heat and the pipes shook and rattled in response. He would have to run to the general store and get some things for the next week like an air mattress and a folding chair. There wasn't even Wi-Fi available.

He went to the window that faced the ocean and threw it open to suck in the salt air. He paused until the gentle sound of the ocean met him.

Where was Liv right now? Probably taking photos of models in crazy outfits and barking out orders to anyone who wouldn't listen to her. He smiled in spite of the ache thoughts of Liv always caused. He had only wanted her to be happy even if that didn't include him. She was the mother of his son. The son who hadn't lived long enough to let his young, dumb dad hold him. If only he'd forced his father to let them hold the baby, maybe then he would've been able to forget about Liv.

He needed to keep his head about him right now. After he went through the attic, he would need to find a job and a direction. Emotions only muddied the waters. His father had been right about that much.

Tonight, he would start to tackle the attic. Tomorrow he'd go to the cemetery. At the end of the week, he would move on. At least in the meantime, he wouldn't bump into Liv around any corner and mess up his chance to get on with his life.

ABOUT THE AUTHOR

From an early age, Stacey Wilk told tales as a way to escape. At six she wrote short stories in composition notebooks, at twelve she wrote a novel on a typewriter, in high school biology she wrote rock star romances in her binder instead of paying attention.

But it wasn't until many years later, inspired by her children and a looming birthday, that she finally took her story-telling seriously. And published her first novel in 2013. Since then, she's gone on to publish fifteen more so women everywhere could fall in love and find an escape of their own.

She isn't done telling stories. Not by a long shot. If you want to read her emotional and honest books about family, romance, and second chances, visit her at www. staceywilk.com

To see what she writes next, follow her Facebook group for her amazing readers – Stacey's Novel Family https://bit.ly/2FK8Lae

Or join her newsletter - https://bit.ly/2A0jEFk

OTHER BOOKS BY STACEY WILK

Winter at the Shore Series
No More Darkness
Light Up0n the Darkness

The Brotherhood Protectors World
Winter's Last Chance
The Last Betrayal
Her Last Word
The Last Days of Christmas
Seduced by Denial
Chill in the Air
Fighting for Tessa
Nash's Promise
Cruz's Watch (coming Feb. 2024)

The Heritage River Series
A Second Chance House
The Bridge Home
The Essence of Whiskey and Tea

The Hometown Series - Candlewood Falls world
Taking Root
Raising Winter

Defining Chances

Beginning Over

Steeling Hearts

Whispering Christmas

Big Sky Country Series

Time Won't Erase

Stay Awhile

Love Never Ends (coming 2024)

The Gabriel Hunter Series (middle grade)

Welcome to Kata-Tartaroo

Welcome to Bibliotheca

Welcome to Skull Mountain